Kalimantan

Also by Lucius Shepard

Green Eyes
The Jaguar Hunter
Life During Wartime
The Ends of the Earth

KALIMANTAN

Lucius Shepard

Illustrated by Jamel Akib

St. Martin's Press
New York

Library of Congress Cataloging-in-Publication Data

Shepard, Lucius.
    Kalimantan / Lucius Shepard.
        p.   cm.
    ISBN 0-312-07007-1
    I. Title.
PS3569.H3939K35   1992
813'.54—dc20   91-34615
                                                                CIP

First published in Great Britain by Random Century Group.

First U.S. Edition: January 1992
10 9 8 7 6 5 4 3 2 1

The quotation on page 7 is from Dom Delillo's novel *The Names*, copyright © 1982. Published by Harvester and Picador, and Alfred A. Knopf and Vintage; reproduced by kind permission.

For Patrick Delahunt

'The nightmare of real things, the fallen wonder of the world . . .'

Don DeLillo
The Names

'MacKinnon was rather a timid man in the beginning,' said Barnett, manipulating a sapphire across the backs of his fingers with a magician's dexterity. 'He evolved into an intemperate man, a dissolute man. Yet it was only towards the end of manhood that he became dangerous.' The sapphire vanished into his hand, and revealing his palm to be empty, he grinned, exposing large yellow teeth that looked as primitive as those of a chimpanzee. 'It wasn't clear initially whether he would turn out to be dangerous to others or merely to himself. However, in this part of the world such niceties of judgement don't count for much. When a danger is perceived, no matter how immature its form, steps are taken to eliminate it before it can develop claws. Usually it's left to men like you and me, foreign devils, to philosophize over the remains. But sometimes we, too, may be called to action by the imperatives of our adopted land. The land, you see, is king in Borneo ... particularly here in Kalimantan. Its dictates command and mould the people, its principles find expression everywhere. Oh, it can be tamed. And someday soon I suppose it will be. There already are sawmills along the rivers, oil rigs islanding the sea. Before long it'll be stripped of magic and rendered devoid of character like most of America and Europe. But so much of it remains in a natural state: as yet it still possesses some of its old powers and compulsions.'

He spoke in Indonesian to the Dayak boy behind the counter at the front of the shop, and the boy began picking over a selection of amethysts, examining them through a jeweller's glass. The curtains drawn across the entranceway twitched, and the seam of leaden light between them thinned. From beyond came the babble of vendors in their boats, passing along the waterways that served as streets in Banjormasim.

'Curtis MacKinnon,' said Barnett reflectively, shifting in his tattered cane chair. His stringy grey hair and leathery, wrinkled face looked too crude to be real, like a mask superimposed on the grainy shadow at his rear. 'You'd never have guessed he'd turn out as he did if you'd seen him when he arrived. Pale and weak, a slug creeping out from the vast unhealthy shadow of America. That was in 'seventy-six. He'd landed a job with Pertamina, the national oil company, doing administrative work on one of the oil rigs. From the occasional visits he paid to the shop, I determined that he was a typical romantic fool, the sort who is usually taught a hard lesson by the realities of the East. In that regard, and in others, I suppose he was not so much different from myself as a young man, though at the time I would have been exercised had anyone suggested a similarity. He would ask all manner of ignorant questions about England – questions I was hard put to answer, because it had been thirty years since I'd seen home. And when I told him that, he looked at me with round eyes and a gaping mouth as if I'd shown him proof of my divinity. 'Thirty years!' he said. 'Christ, there couldn't have been *anything* here back then.' Well, I told him that was hardly the case, but he was intent on making me out a pioneer, on believing I'd had a hand in conquering the savage land.

'I recall he used to paw through my stock of sapphires, searching for black ones. The blues were of better quality, but being unfamiliar, the black stones were talismans to him, evidence of the distance he'd put between himself and the uninspired reality of his home. It was plain from our talks that he'd read his Conrad, his Maugham, and that he'd ignored the despairing tone of their work and extracted only the mystery, the exoticism. I could just picture him as a boy, lying in bed and whispering the magical names of Kuala Lumpur, Singapore, Surabaya, and imagining himself lost among them. He looked upon

Kalimantan as a place in which a man could fall under a dark enchantment, and I think he believed that kind of destiny was somehow virtuous, a resolution to the problem of being an American in the midst of so much chaotic change and poverty. A feeble moral attitude, I grant you, but at least it embodied a morality of sorts, which is more than most expatriates will express in regard to Kalimantan. That attitude may have played a part in his downfall – and it could be that what happened was related to a form of cowardice. I've known quite a few men who've hoped disaster would strike them, or that the tropics would expose a seam of weakness and infect them in some mortal way in order that they might evade responsibility for their lives. And yet sitting here today I can't be sure that any of MacKinnon's wishes or predilections were true determinants of his fate.'

It wasn't until four years after he'd arrived – he was about thirty, then – that I became involved with him. He'd left Pertamina under a cloud. Rumours of shortages and so forth. And he'd entered into the black market. I heard that he'd got into drug running, and I knew for a fact he was importing Thai women to serve as wives for the Arab workers in the oil fields. There was nothing illegal about this last, but it smacked of slavery to the western community, and tales were carried about the women being used to bring in contraband. MacKinnon's appearance had changed a great deal. He'd lost his pudginess and grown into a tanned, rawboned fellow with ragged black hair and hollowed cheeks always dirtied by stubble, and hazel eyes shaded by thick brows. All in all, a somewhat sinister face. But its sinister effect was diminished, made into something boyish by the petulant set of his mouth. His voice was hoarse from clove cigarettes and as a result had a menacing softness that he used to inspire caution in the scum with whom he dealt. He was ever careful to let them know that despite his core of American innocence, he was capable, as capable as they, of bloodshed. But I

11

knew this was a sham. He was still an innocent, and that to me was his central puzzle: how the dishonourable acts he committed had left that core of innocence untouched. Was the process of his decline, his going-to-seed, imbued with such a deliberate romanticism that it invested his life with the quality of a performance and allowed him to disregard the very real consequences that attended his actions, the carrying-out of his role? So it seemed to me. Yet I may be overstating the case and its contrasts, and thus drawing inaccurate conclusions. MacKinnon, you see, was no absolute villain. He cheated and he swindled, but did so with an economy and style that impressed even the local swindlers. Indeed, it might be said that he brought an accent of civilized stability to the milieu of the petty criminal in these parts.

He had been born in Florida, a place of which he rarely spoke. To his mind, I think, it was a fraudulent tropic, utterly shadowed by the real one to which he had travelled. He'd suffered a typical American upbringing, typical in accord with the fact that the role of the family there has been reduced to that of a centrifuge, its erratic spin flinging off children who rarely return home from the random directions in which they have been flung. That emptiness at the heart of his life was, I'm certain, instrumental in shaping his personality; he saw emptiness in every incidence of fullness and so could never be satisfied with what he had, always searching for something that would overwhelm or consume him. For no reason other than a minor talent at maths, he had enrolled in the engineering programme at Georgia Tech, and, following graduation, he took a position with an oil company in Louisiana where, as he put it, he excelled at errorless mediocrity. And so, with no love in his life, no real aim, he reinvented the unsatisfied love and aim of his childhood – to wander, to be disreputable and lost – and came at last to Kalimantan, where hosts of the disreputable and lost had gathered in the spirit of commerce to celebrate the rape of sea and forest.

13

In 1980, on the night the drilling platform off Bontang was destroyed, that was when our relationship, such as it was, began in earnest. Built out over the harbour at Bontang is an immense wharf, upon which is situated a complex of bars and brothels and restaurants that cater to the riggers and to the loggers who work the timberlands along the Mahakam River. It's fascinating, in that there you get a sense of the cultural syncretism taking place in the area. Dayaks, a generation removed from head-hunting, wearing designer jeans and wrist-watches; Arabs in burnouses and *jellabas*; tall, tanned Americans and Australians. I'd gone there to sell a diamond to one of the riggers, and after the sale had been accomplished I strolled out towards the end of the wharf, out past the neons and the music. It was a perfect night, as perfect, at any rate, as nights are likely to get in a country where the mercury rarely dips below ninety. There were not many stars, most obscured by thin clouds. But there was a moon. A great round silver seal of a moon stamped high and central in the dark, transforming the untroubled sea into an infinite black cloth sewn with a billion sequins. The drilling platform was a mechanical spider with intricate towers and spans of web in silhouette against a starless band of sky that some thickness in the air had turned a dusky purple. A man in an orange-and-maroon batik jacket, and a Thai woman with long black hair and a dress of green silk were standing at the railing, gazing towards the platform, and, as I drew near, I recognized MacKinnon. The two of them were deep in conversation – by all appearances, an agitated conversation. MacKinnon gripped the railing with one hand and gestured wildly with the other. I could hear bits and pieces of what he was saying. 'Why did . . .?' and 'I'm sick of . . .' He started to walk away, but she caught his arm and pulled him back. At that moment the platform exploded.

It was odd, the sharpness of my perceptions then. Not only did I register the horrid particulars of the explosion, the concussion that sheared off the drift of music from

14

the bars, the gout of flame like a rip in the blackness, the sections of tower thrown out in arcs, the secondary explosions spraying meteoric swarms of fiery debris, but I also registered every reaction displayed by MacKinnon and the woman. He staggered back, arms upflung as if to ward off the wreckage falling into the sea, and I had no doubt that he had been taken completely by surprise. The woman, however, stood stockstill, staring at the blaze as if calmed by the sight. The wind blew her hair all to one side, a shape in miniature identical to the plume of fire blowing sideways from the broken pipe sunk into the ocean floor. Screams and cries of alarm began to sound from the bars. MacKinnon grabbed the woman by her shoulders and seemed to be questioning her. She kept shaking her head. 'Goddamn you!' he shouted. He drew back his hand to strike her, but spotted me watching them. His distraught expression changed to one of anger, and he started towards me, intending, I assumed, some violence; but instead he veered away and sprinted off into the crowd of drunken labourers and whores that had gathered behind us, their sweaty faces agleam with the brilliance of the burning platform. I watched him vanish among them, and when I turned back to the railing I discovered that the woman, too, had fled.

The next day a splinter Communist group took responsibility for the explosion. I had supposed that it had been no accident, and further, I couldn't help but relate the presence of MacKinnon and the Thai woman to the disaster. There was no hard evidence of a connection, but when I replayed those moments in my mind, I kept seeing connections in the peculiar ways in which they had reacted. Why, for instance, had MacKinnon been angry with her after his shock had eroded? In the light of such a tragedy, I doubted he would have been continuing a lovers' quarrel. The more I thought about it, the more certain I became that the explosion had represented for him an unexpected evolution of events. And then there was the woman's evident lack of surprise, the rapidity

15

with which they both had left the scene. It was difficult to believe that these reactions did not signal some sort of guilty involvement.

I was about to close for the evening three days later when MacKinnon came into the shop. He had on the same sports jacket he'd worn that night on the wharf, and from the condition of his clothing, his heavy growth of beard and general unsteadiness, I had the impression that he had not slept for some time. He entered with a swagger, but on meeting my eyes he deflated, all his arrogance turning to an air of distraction. He plucked at the sleeve of his jacket, cast about for something unchallenging at which to stare, and then, squaring his shoulders, asked how I'd been. I was certain that he'd had it in mind to say something entirely different, but I didn't press the matter and limited myself to an exchange of pleasantries. I watched him move about the shop, picking up stones, holding them to the light. After a few minutes of this, he pulled a large uncut red diamond from his pocket, a stone of perhaps thirty carats. 'What'll you give me?' he asked as I examined it. I named a figure, an extremely low figure, and was surprised that he didn't attempt to haggle, saying that he needed the money at once, that he had to leave for Hong Kong. I took this for evidence that the diamond had been stolen, and I examined it again. It was quite a windfall at the price, and under other circumstances I would have paid quickly and got him out of there before he could change his mind. What stopped me from that course? Not friendship, certainly. And not curiosity. I would like to believe that I apprehended some rare potential in the moment, that I saw in him my younger self and was for that reason sympathetic; but I am convinced that this was merely an incidence of the debased lowlife in us all, the sense we have of another's profound helplessness that persuades us to suspend normal judgements and pretend kindness, when all we are really doing is taking advantage of a moment in which we can exercise control and indulge in a feeling of power.

16

I told him I'd be happy to give him the money, but it seemed that trouble had set its hooks in him. Perhaps it was none of my business, I said, but it had occurred to me that money might not be the answer to his problems. Sometimes, I told him, a friendly ear was the only edge a man could gain over whatever was harrowing him; sometimes talking steadied the floor under one's feet and made a man hold back from precipitate action. I said far more than that, using my words to feel about for a grip on him, to probe for a response, and those particular comments were the ones that appeared the most effective. He walked to the door, watching his feet as if measuring off the paces, and from the tension in his pose I expected him to bolt. But he stopped and peered out through the curtains at the twilit waters. 'I've been set up,' he said. He turned and came back to the counter. 'It wasn't the Communists who blew up the platform. It was Pertamina.'

I didn't believe him at first, but he went on to explain that Pertamina had approached him with the idea of running a sting operation on the Communists, involving them in a large drug transaction with the Vietnamese, whom the run of Indonesians despised, and thus tarnishing their populist appeal. They offered to wipe out his bad record, to establish him in a legitimate and lucrative business, as well as give him a sizeable cash reward. Ordinarily, he said, he would have rejected the offer, but of late he had been reassessing his goals, his life, and the thought of making a new start had appealed to him. They'd guaranteed that he would be in no personal danger and had provided him with bodyguards so that he would feel secure when dealing with the Communists; but he had come to realize that he had been manipulated by the bodyguards, manoeuvred through a chain of events whose effect had been to make it appear that he was in a leadership position with the insurgency. He'd been on the run since the explosion and had been informed by friends inside Pertamina that he would soon be implicated in order to sway public opinion against the United States; leftist elements in the company felt that if they could demonstrate American interference in national affairs, this would initiate a new direction in foreign policy.

'Jesus, what have I been doing?' he said, glancing up to the ceiling as if hoping a light would shine down. He shook his head ruefully and rested his hands on the counter. 'You know, it's fucking amazing how you can go along thinking you've got the world by the short hairs, and then you get smacked in the stones and realize you never had a clue.' He shook his head again. 'Not a fucking clue.'

'When you started dealing drugs,' I said, 'what was on your mind? What was your plan?'

He shot me a perplexed look. 'What's that got to do with anything?'

'I'm just curious as to how much you don't understand about this country,' I said. 'But you don't have to humour me.'

He held my eyes, and in that moment I realized I was his one hope, his court of last appeal. His friends were untrustworthy, and so he had come to someone whom he scarcely knew. I couldn't help feeling sympathy for him, even though he was only another American fool betrayed by a belief in the invulnerability of his national armour, his faith in the immunity offered by a sophisticated overview of the supposedly primitive culture in which he had chosen to live.

'I think I wanted to impress myself,' he said. 'To feel like I was a badass, but still a good guy at heart. In here' – he tapped his forehead – 'it's as if I've been living in a comic book. I've finally waked up to that.'

I'm not sure why, but my sympathy was fully enlisted now. Perhaps the fact that he had reached the point of desperation, where honesty was his only option . . . perhaps because I was so unaccustomed to honesty, this had a poignant effect upon me. I recalled some lines from Conrad: 'A man who is born is like a man who has jumped into the sea. If he tries to climb out into the air as inexperienced people do, he drowns.' Well, I was MacKinnon's fellow in this particular sea, and I knew that if he continued on his present course he would drown in the rich air of the East. I alone could save him.

'You'll be better off staying here,' I said. 'The thing to do is to head upriver and lose yourself in the hills 'til all this blows over.'

He gave a despairing laugh. 'That won't be for a hell of a long time.'

'You're absolutely right,' I said. 'Years, most likely. But they'll be years of life, of freedom. And if what you're telling me is accurate, should you try to leave Kalimantan, you'll probably be captured. You know they'll be laying for you. If they get their hands on you, they won't be merciful.'

'I have no choice,' he said. 'I don't know a damn thing about Dayak country.'

I wasn't altogether certain that I wanted to risk myself against the minions of Pertamina, but I was borne along by a charitable momentum. 'I do,' I said. 'I'll help you.'

In exchange for the diamond (I didn't allow myself to be wholly charitable) I supplied MacKinnon with false documents and had him smuggled upriver, first to Lognawan in Dayak territory and then to a trading post some two-weeks' walk into the hill country. The post was operated by an old friend, Paul Tenzer, a Dutch zoologist who had lived in Borneo for the past forty-five years. I had communicated with Tenzer by radio and worked out an agreement that guaranteed MacKinnon's keep. MacKinnon was to serve as Tenzer's secretary, and I was to compensate Tenzer in relation to how well he performed his duties. Tenzer was a crusty old man, and I could not imagine that the relationship between he and MacKinnon would be other than thorny. Yet for the following two years, harmony ensued. I received monthly letters from Tenzer, and each featured some

19

tribute to MacKinnon's character. The most startling of these tributes were contained in letters dated 14 October 1982 and December 29 of that same year.

'It astonishes me to recall,' Tenzer wrote, 'that, when Curtis arrived, I doubted he would be able to cope with either the simplicity of the human condition hereabouts or the intricate oppressiveness of the wild. He was a man of the cities, I thought, and would always remain so. Yet during the past year, particularly in the past few months, he has undergone an amazing transformation. Gone is the pallor, the indifferent health, the slovenliness of mind. He seems a man of this place now. Alert, strong, analytical as regards the dangers and potentials of the jungle. Not only has he proven a great help in my work, he has also undertaken work of his own. I'm not sure what this work entails as he is being secretive about it; he says he wishes to surprise me. But he goes about it with great zeal, spending long hours in the jungle, working sometimes late into the night. Often we will sit of an evening and talk over a bottle of wine. I find these conversations stimulating, but more importantly, I am heartened to see how stimulating they are to him. It is as if he is coming out of a long darkness, a sinner passing through cleansing fire. That metaphor may strike you as excessive, but were you to ask him how he felt about all that has happened to him here, I am certain he would couch his answer in evangelical terms. He believes that by some sinister and unlikely course he has reached the place that he was always meant to be.'

Then the second letter:

'How grateful I am, my old friend, that you have sent Curtis to me! I've never hoped that my work would achieve more than minimal success, but now at least I have had the honour of shepherding the truly innovative. I realize you may think me mad on reading this, but I firmly believe that the name of Curtis MacKinnon will one day be celebrated as that of a genius and will be spoken in the same breath as the names Leonardo and Einstein. I cannot speak of the work he is doing. He has asked me

20

to be discreet, and in truth my understanding of it is not sufficient to render a clear explanation. But suffice it to say that it is radical and borders upon the miraculous.'

In the letters that followed, Tenzer made only incidental references to 'the work', and my curiosity – which had been piqued by his enthusiastic pronouncements – abated. I assumed that either he had erred in his initial judgment concerning the value of MacKinnon's researches or that he was engaging in some covert game, one that might well be the product of senility. He was, after all, in his mid-seventies, and such a tragic slippage was to be expected.

The letters continued to arrive with regularity over the next year and a half, and although I maintained my interest in MacKinnon, I relegated him to the status of old news. But there came a day in April when I received a brief note from Tenzer that changed all that:

'It is a matter of utmost urgency that you come to see me as soon as possible. I dare not commit more to paper, but be assured this is no trivial request. Please come, my old friend, and do not be frightened of the things you may see in the country beyond Longnawan. You will not be harmed.'

MacKinnon had added a postscript, seconding Tenzer's plea, and this as much as the note persuaded me to pay attention to the summons, for in almost four years, although he had conveyed his respects through Tenzer, he had not once written me.

It proved impossible to communicate with the trading post by radio, and I debated whether or not to go. I was getting a bit long in the tooth for jungle travel, and perhaps that was the crucial factor in my decision: the realization that if I didn't take this opportunity I might not have another. I spent several days in settling my affairs – I was anticipating a trip of several weeks' duration – and then booked my passage from Tenggarong up the Mahakam river on a stubby little vessel that vented plumes of black smoke and greatly resembled *The African Queen*. From Longnawan I set out on foot into the hill

21

country with a Dayak guide named Madwe, who was travelling to a village near the trading post to marry a local girl. He was a wiry fellow in his thirties with a catlike delicacy to his features, and skin the colour of teakwood. There were intricate tattoos on his chest and arms, heavy silver earrings had elongated the lobes of his ears so that they hung down to his jawline, and his teeth were stained reddish-black from chewing *sirih* and betelnut. He dressed in tattered chinos, a soiled white shirt, and an old fisherman's hat. In a mesh straw basket strapped to his back he carried gifts for his bride and her family, and strapped to his belt were a blowgun and a long-bladed knife with an enamelled hilt shaped like a bird's foot. He was – like most of his people – an amiable sort, and his company brought to mind my youthful travels with other guides and thus gave me the feeling of having dropped more than a few years. The land itself had that same effect upon me. It had been too long since I had touched the soul of Kalimantan, and now, being once again in that secret heartland, I understood anew my fascination with Borneo. Standing one morning atop a hill some nine days out from Longnawan, I overlooked a sombre green sea of other hills, with a winding river glinting like a strand of tinsel under the strong sun, and here and there the tawny island of a clearing, menaced by the towering waves of the jungle, and in the middle distance the dark punctuation of the village towards which we were heading – it would be the three-quarter mark of our journey. The silence and stillness were oppressive in their force, seeming a wall I had run up against, one that not even the light could fully penetrate – as if the land were a kind of deep, a trench that absorbed all radiance and transformed it into an entirely new element imbued with the unique and mysterious nature of the place. And despite my belief that Kalimantan was doomed, destined to be overflown by tourists in helicopters, with jungle Hiltons and monkey-spotting tours, I understood then that the place still had its defences, that it would take a formidable force, indeed, to penetrate and corrupt this last of the wild.

Darkness fell before we could reach the village, which was called Tanjung Segar, and we camped a mile or so to the east in a clearing bordered by secondary growth and banks of ferns. Mist lowered about us, and our cooking fire took on a phantom aspect, the flames showing pale, appearing to writhe with a slow, lascivious torsion like the movements of fiery dancers. The mist muffled all sound. Even the condensation dripping from the leaves was more an intensified absence than a noise, an incessant dimpling in the stillness. Underlit by the fire, the crown of a palm leaning in above looked like the headdress of an enormous savage, its body hidden by the dark. As we waited for sleep, Madwe offered me a handful of *sirih* leaves, which contained a mild narcotic. Their taste was bitter, but after a while the haloed fire, the sparkling atoms of mist, the shadowy vegetation, all that came to seem a cosy frame for my thoughts, their rhythms as sensuous as those of the flames. Yet I could not escape the feeling that some evil was afoot. And when I caught Madwe staring at me, his face strained, in a panic I asked, 'What is it?'

After a long pause he said, 'Something is here.'

For the moment I was too stoned, too full of belief in the mystic potentials of the night, to doubt him. 'What do you mean . . . something?'

He appeared to be listening to some signal inaudible to me. 'I don't know,' he said. He lowered his head as if in concentration. 'Something . . .' He let out a sigh. 'It is gone now. It was not hunting us.'

I was ashamed of myself for having let his anxiety derail my good sense; he had obviously fallen prey to some superstitious impulse, and I felt secure in the light of his primitive reactions. 'We're perfectly safe, Madwe,' I said with a chuckle.

He looked at me in that beatific way the Dayaks exhibit when they have given up communicating with westerners and don't wish to perturb them. 'I know,' he said. 'We are safe, now.'

The next morning I woke before Madwe. Although the mist was still thick, it did not seem ominous, but beautiful and serene. Dawn was a bluish-green effusion of light, the sun a sickly pallor in the east above the vague slate-blue outlines of the hills. I pissed onto a fern bank, the splash of my urine an affirmation of human reality in all that mystical instability. Then I walked along the path that led towards Tanjung Segar, pressing through ferns and dew-hung cobwebs and trailing vines, emerging from the jungle onto a ledge overlooking a gorge that separated the hill where we had camped from that upon which the village was situated. The gorge was spanned by an old rickety suspension bridge of rope and planks that extended from a clump of shadowy palms out over a void of bluish-white haze and vanished into the brush on the far side some forty yards farther along. From where I stood it had the look of a narrow mesh of cobweb stretched to the breaking point. The bridge's fragile structure mounted against the diffuse reach of the sky imbued the scene with an infinite air, as if this were a last human construct beyond which lay the uncreate; and assisting in this impression, lending both perspective and scale, was the silhouetted figure of a man who was standing at the bridge's mid-point, gripping one of the ropes that served for a railing. At that distance, in that murk, I should not have been able to identify the figure, yet I knew it was MacKinnon. How I knew this, I'm not clear. By his stance, perhaps, or by some more subtle signal. But the knowledge was unshakable. And the sense I had that he could see me, despite the fact that I would be invisible to the normal eye against the backdrop of the jungle, was frightening in the extreme. Was he waiting for me? How could he have timed his appearance on the bridge to coincide with my arrival? I had the idea that the silence had deepened, that an inaudible vibration –

like a racing pulse – was beating towards me from that motionless dark figure, and I shrank back into the foliage. A moment later I peered between the leaves. MacKinnon, if it had been he, was gone.

I couldn't have lost sight of him for more than a few seconds, and considering the bridge's dilapidated condition, which forced one to move cautiously from plank to plank, he would not have been able to walk from the centre to either end in so short a time. The only way he could have vanished would have been to jump . . . Or perhaps he had never been there. That, I thought, was the most likely possibility, that I was still under the influence of the *sirih*, and as I retraced my path I began to deny what had seemed undeniable at the bridge.

The mist did not lift, and when Madwe and I approached Tanjung Segar an hour later the faces carved on the phallic totems that guarded the outskirts of the village looked all the more fearsome, their deformed features and painted teeth and protruding tongues appearing through rips in the mist and then fading. Straw baskets full of garbage were hung on pegs beneath the faces, and the clammy stink that arose from them was a greater deterrent than the fierce expressions above. Beyond the totems, the longhouses, with their high-peaked, swaybacked thatched roofs and blank windows, resembled ghostly galleons riding in a sea of fog. We had not proceeded fifty feet into the village when I realized it was deserted. Communal pots had been overturned, their contents spilled and gone rancid; articles of clothing and various personal possessions were strewn across the packed dirt. The emptiness beat at me with the slow resonance of a gong. Madwe called out in Dayak, but received no response. He stood with his head tipped to the side, his right hand on the hilt of his knife. The back of my neck prickled, and I assigned malevolent sources to the drips and rustles that came to my ear. Mist was accumulating in a dense band above the rooftops, gathering into a menagerie of greyish-green shapes, and visibility was poor even at ground level.

26

Through the drifting veils of condensation, the carvings on the lintel and porch and pilings of the house facing us – their intricacy testifying that this was the *waidan*'s (female shaman's) dwelling – appeared to be writhing. The silence was so thick, it seemed capable of muting a scream into a whisper. Madwe drew his knife, and I unholstered my sidearm. Then we moved towards the *waidan*'s house and cautiously negotiated the short ladder that led up to the door.

The odour of rotten fruit was strong within, as was the cloying sweetness that results from too many people living at close quarters. The windows were covered, and the wan light from the doorway did little to erode the darkness. Madwe told me to switch on my torch. I fumbled it out of my pack and began a slow sweep of the room, illuminating straw mats littered with cooking implements and beadwork, a bolt of fabric. I had the feeling I was being watched; the same rapid pulse I had sensed at the bridge was in the air. But the room was empty. I swung the light up onto the walls, the ceiling. The beam tracked across rafters carved with friezes of animal faces and fruit. Then, as I inspected the vault between the rafters, the beam revealed a disembodied human face that looked to be floating in mid-air like an image projected onto the darkness. It was unmistakably the face of a *waidan*, a grinning hag with black, filed teeth and gleaming eyes, framed by brambles of grey hair. I held the torch steady, too stunned to move. But then the face dissolved . . . dissolved into a scatter of dusky particles that came flowing down into the beam of light and into the torch itself. The metal cylinder jerked in my hand, possessed, I assumed, by the essence of that hideous face. With a shout, I flung it aside and bolted. I scrambled down the ladder, Madwe close behind, and tripped on the bottom rung, going flat on my back. My head struck the ground hard, and for an instant I was dazed, my vision blurred. I rolled over, rubbing the back of my neck. Madwe was crouched beside me, peering at the sky, his mouth open,

27

the ligature of his neck cabled; and when I saw what had caught his eye, I too sat gaping and unable to move.

I have said that prior to entering the longhouse the mist had been accumulating above the rooftops, boiling into convulsed shapes – not an unusual development. But while we had been inside, those half-formed shapes had been fully realized, and now, hovering overhead were immense semblances of the demons carved on the village totems. They towered fifty feet high, leering faces with fangs and waggling tongues and distended eyes, all cunningly wrought of varying thicknesses of mist. The wind had picked up, but although the faces rippled like seaweed lifting on a swell, they held their shapes and positions, fixing us with mad stares. I was afraid, yet so thoroughly dominated by the eerie presences in the sky, I was ready to accept whatever would happen, and I waited in a luminous calm for death to take me. But the misty faces kept their distance, and at length I got to my feet and urged Madwe to stand. He was trembling, clutching a charm that dangled from a thong about his neck, and I knew he was on the verge of collapse. I recalled Tenzer's note, his admonition that I should not be afraid of things seen along the way, and that reassured me somewhat. Steering Madwe by the arm, I started towards the jungle with a faltering step, keeping my eyes lowered, not wanting to see what changes, if any, the enormous faces were undergoing. I didn't turn back until we had gone fifty yards beyond the outskirts, and when I did I found that the mist had thinned and the faces had been absorbed back into their fathering medium.

With three days walk ahead of us, eleven if we were to turn back, it made no sense to return to Longnawan, and we decided to push forward at once and put as much distance as possible between ourselves and Tanjung Segar – though judging by the contents of Tenzer's note, I doubted what we had witnessed was a localized phenomenon. And I was right in this. Not two hours later, we pushed through a stand of bamboo and came face to face with an extraordinary tiger, its fur pure white with stripes as indistinct as smudged charcoal lines, and its eyes the piercing blue of fine gemstones; it leaped toward us and vanished in mid-air. There were apparitions everywhere throughout the jungle. Ghostly beasts; warriors in devil masks; a stream that ran with blood; strange chants that issued from above as if from phantom tribes in the mist. We encountered dozens of such curiosities, and we encountered them with increasing frequency as the day wore on. But although they continued to inspire awe, I learned to accept them without fear. Despite their horrific nature, I recognized some to be elements of the folklore of Kalimantan, and once I realized that they would do me no harm, I began to look forward to seeing more. It appeared that the land itself was in an excited state, yielding up its mythic potentials, its ghosts and demons, in a hallucinated flourish, and I suspected – no matter how unfounded my suspicion, or how improbable it seemed – that all this must be related to MacKinnon's researches. What that portended was beyond me, and why my presence would be required at the trading post now struck me as more perplexing than before.

We camped that evening on a hilltop overlooking other lesser hills. The sky was clear, a deep royal blue in colour, and there was a half-moon low on the horizon. It was so bright that I could make out the separate shapes of the crowns of the trees on the distant hills. And it grew brighter yet. Shooting stars, a profusion such as I had never seen, streaked down and disappeared behind the hills, and – flying in the face of all expectation – a hellish red glow appeared in the east, accompanied by a rumbling that issued from the earth beneath my feet. Every now and again the rumbling would intensify, and a gout of flaming stuff would hurtle aross the sky and fall into the jungle, setting it ablaze. At least so it appeared, though the fires did not last more than a few minutes. No active volcanoes existed in the region, and even if one had, an eruption could not have materialized with such suddenness. Yet there it was, and this primaeval sight affected me more powerfully than any of the previous illusions. Cold knotted in my groin, and my stomach contracted. I glanced over at Madwe. He was sitting cross-legged, his face glowing in the firelight, his eyesockets and the creases in his skin filled with shadow, and he was staring at the volcano without expression, like a man in a dream. Behind him, a spray of shooting stars slit fiery seams down the sky.

'Madwe?' I said, thinking that he might be more a part of this than I and have intimate knowledge concerning it. 'Do you know what the hell is happening here?'

After a pause, without turning his head or shifting his eyes towards me, he said, 'In Longnawan there is a woodcarver named Manggis. When you return, will you have him build my canoe?'

'What are you talking about, man?'

'Have him carve it in the shape of a watersnake, and pay him with the gifts in my basket.'

I understood then that he was asking me to commission his burial canoe. 'Don't be an idiot!' I said. 'You're not going to die.'

He made no reply.

'Madwe!' I said.

He remained silent, motionless, his eyes fixed on the east.

I gave up trying to talk to him and settled back on my sleeping bag, my own courage boosted by his fear; I would have to be responsible for him, I realized, and help him overcome his primitive reactions. The pyrotechnic display in the sky continued, and I thought it must have looked this same way millions of years before during the Cenozoic. I watched for a very long time, and even after I closed my eyes, streams of fire scored the darkness behind my lids. I imagined I was seeing the whirling of great scythes and wheels of flame, creations ever more brilliant and fantastic; and when at last I fell asleep, rather than sinking into the clamour of dreams, I felt

I was rising higher and higher into realms of silent light.

I woke the next day thinking that someone had called to me, but there was no one about other than Madwe, who was sitting in the same position as he had been when I had fallen asleep. The fire was ashes, and the volcano in the east had been replaced by the sunrise, a crimson smear that fanned across the horizon. I stretched, shook out the kinks and said good morning to Madwe, but, as had happened the night before, he gave no response.

'For God's sake!' I said. 'Stop this nonsense!'

I nudged him, and he wobbled, but maintained his pose. His skin was infused with a pallor, except for his fingers, which were unnaturally dark, betraying the fact that his blood had settled. He had clearly been dead for several hours. I sat wondering at what had apparently been a surrender of will, thinking that the next few days would not be pleasant. I did not want to look away from Madwe, less afraid of the aspect of death than of the sweep of jungle that lay between the hilltop and the trading post, for I felt that, despite the miles already travelled, with no one for company, no conversation to impede the contagion of fear, my true journey might have just begun.

My first sight of the trading post had upon me the stirring effect of a pilgrim's first glimpse of his central mystery. The previous seventy-two hours had left me with a new appreciation for the virtues of companionship, and, when I spotted the peak of Tenzer's tin roof between the trees, I hurried towards it, tearful with relief. But when I emerged from the underbrush and had a clear view of the compound, I realized that, instead of having escaped the madness of the jungle, I had penetrated to its insane heart. The compound had been erected in a burned-off clearing among mahogany trees and was surrounded by a fifteen-foot-high fence of pitch-coated trunks lashed together by thick cable and sharpened into stakes. The last time I had seen it, the fence had been unadorned,

but now epiphytes with orchidaceous blooms had been braided together and draped across it, forming a wall of flowers and green leaves, and hundreds of snakeskins had been nailed to the wood, creating a rotting fly-swarmed fringe at the base. Through the half-open gate I could see that the roofs of the two houses were populated by hundreds of birds, perhaps a thousand all told, and they were setting up a racket that outvoiced the rattle of the generator; the air was thick with butterflies, fluttering and dancing like multi-coloured snow. There was so much movement within the compound that the jungle with its winded leaves seemed frozen by contrast. I stood before the gate, uncertain whether to go forward or to flee. Despite the butterflies and the birds, the place had a deserted air that made me increasingly leery. The noise of the birds swelled in volume, becoming a chaotic gabbling, and that influenced my decision. But as I turned back to the jungle a voice called out, 'Barnett!'

A long-haired, bearded man in jeans and a loose white shirt had appeared beside the gate. He came towards me, walking easily, his arms a-swing, head tipped to one side as if trying to see me at an angle that would provide maximum clarity. It was MacKinnon, of course. I knew him at once. But that knowledge, rather than staunching my fear, intensified it. Suddenly all the fragmentary details concerning him in Tenzer's letters – his work, his noble transformation – seemed articles of menace, and his casual approach struck me as emblematic of a malefic power, not of friendly intent. I backed away, ready to bolt, but my heel caught on something, a root, a stone, and I went sprawling, my hands clutching at the air.

'What the fuck's wrong with you?' he said as he came up. 'Aren't you glad to see me?' He reached out and hauled me to my feet, took a step back and gazed at me admiringly. 'You're looking pretty good for an old fart.'

All this time I had been trying to read his face, to detect an essential attitude, some quality that would reveal his secret disposition, the alien nature I felt must underly

33

his power; but while he gave the impression of being healthier and more confident than the man I had known in Banjormasim, he appeared normal in every respect.

'You'll have to forgive me,' I said. 'The trip . . .'

'Hell of a light show, huh?' He chuckled. 'Well, you're home free now, man. So loosen up.'

'The light show,' I said. 'Was that your doing?'

He nodded, less an affirmation than a contemplative gesture. 'Yeah, I guess.'

'You guess?' I said. 'I don't understand how anyone could be unclear about their responsibility for the things I've been seeing.'

'I don't much understand it, either,' he said good-naturedly, and draped an arm over my shoulder. 'You must be exhausted. Let's get you situated.'

I pulled away. 'Where's Tenzer?'

'In the house. I'll let him explain things to you . . . At least, his side of it.' He gazed off into the jungle. 'I'm afraid what's happened has affected him badly. He's not the man he used to be. Keep that in mind.'

'It hasn't affected me very well, either,' I said. 'Why did he want me here, anyway? And why did you?'

'You're the only man who's ever given me good advice,' he said. 'And now I need advice. That why I intercepted Tenzer's note and added my two-cents' worth.' He glanced down at the ground, scuffed it with his toe. 'As for what he wants, Tenzer . . . I imagine he wants you to stop me.'

'Stop you?' I said. 'Stop you from what?'

He let out a grunt that might have been a laugh. 'I'm not sure.'

The houses within the compound were – like Dayak houses – set on pilings, but there all resemblance ended. The walls were of white stucco, the roofs of red tile. Like cosy bungalows that had sprouted spindly legs. As we approached the larger of the two, the clamour of the birds stilled and the butterflies eddied away from us, a turn of events that played upon my nerves, and I felt easier after we had negotiated the stairs. It was dark inside, the room cooled by a slowly circulating ceiling fan; the light, sliced by bamboo blinds, illuminated strips of a large room with hardwood floors and straw mats and wicker chairs and a desk piled high with notebooks, papers and folios. In the panes of specimen cases stacked high along one wall were sections of our opaque reflections, much as we might have appeared to the compound eye of a giant insect. Hundreds of shoe boxes, each marked with a pencilled designation, were stacked along the other walls, and in the gloom I could make out the occasional cryptic legend: IBA FUNERAL and ECLIPSE, LENAWESIN and PUNAN DAYAK. That last inscription aroused my curiosity. The Punan Dayak had been nomads, dwelling in the most inaccessible parts of the jungle, following the tides of game, and, according to the conventional wisdom, they were extinct. They had been known as the 'dream wanderers' and were rumoured to travel in trance-states beyond the borders of this world to a place where horned serpents lived in the rivers and stranger beasts yet occupied the deep jungle. It had once been a dream of mine and Tenzer's to find the Punan Dayak, to prove that they still existed; we had thought of them as emblems of wilderness, of Kalimantan's ancient purity and magic, and while I had long since given up on the idea, considering it to be a symptom of the deluded romanticism of youth, Tenzer, if the shoe box was of any significance, had apparently maintained an interest in the tribe.

I was about to lift this particular shoe box from its niche, when from behind me came the sound of scraping, dragging footsteps; the next moment a stooped figure appeared in the doorway to a corridor that led deeper into the house.

'Barnett! Thank God!' Tenzer's voice was whispery, dry, almost toneless, like a voice simulated by the artful rubbing together of dead leaves. He advanced a few paces into the room, leaning heavily on a cane. He was a lean

35

old man, his grey hair as long as MacKinnon's: an old wizard in safari gear, with a hooked nose and cadaverous cheeks and blue eyes so widely spaced that they lent his face a permanent expression of mild astonishment. His right hand atop the cane resembled a pale knotted root. He peered at me, then shifted his gaze to MacKinnon, who was standing at my shoulder, adopting a reproving look that reminded me of the way my father had once regarded me in those moments when he had perceived me as his great failure.

'I'll leave you to talk,' said MacKinnon.

Tenzer acknowledged this with the slightest of nods. Once MacKinnon had gone, he invited me to sit, and, with much laborious breathing, lowered himself into the chair behind the desk. He fussed with papers and asked after my health. I told him I was well and asked him to explain what was going on; but he motioned me to silence, and we limited ourselves to small talk until the birds on the roof renewed their clamour.

'We can talk now,' Tenzer said, implying what I had half assumed, that the birds had been quieted by MacKinnon's presence in the compound, and also that MacKinnon's hearing was far superior to that of a normal man. Although I had made this assumption, I didn't wholly accept it and, even after Tenzer had verified it, I was tempted to believe that Tenzer in his dotage had lapsed into fantasy. My head was aswarm with thoughts, none of which connected in logical sequence, and I asked him once again to explain the things I had been seeing.

'I know part of it,' he said. 'But only a small part. I doubt even Curtis knows it all.' He clasped his hands, tapped his forefingers against his lips. 'Were you aware of Curtis's heroin addiction?'

'Heroin?' I said. 'I had no idea.'

'He had a serious dependency when he arrived,' said Tenzer. 'He'd brought quite a supply with him, and while I knew he was using it, I raised no objection. I merely pointed out that he had no way of obtaining more – not on a regular basis, at any rate. He was very reasonable about it. He knew he would have to withdraw sooner or later, and he was constantly trying to find some means of easing the process. He tapered off, preparing as best he could for the inevitable. That alone caused him intense physical suffering, and I suggested that one of the local *waidans* might have something more potent than *sirih*, something that would act as a surrogate. The locals couldn't do much for him, but they told him he should consult the *waidan* of Tanjung Segar, who was very powerful, very wise.'

'Oh, Lord!' I said, and filled Tenzer in on what I'd seen in the village. He registered little reaction until I mentioned the apparition of the *waidan*'s face; then he clenched his fists and looked up at the ceiling.

'Is the *waidan* dead?' I asked.

'You'll have to ask Curtis,' he said. 'But I suspect as much.' He let out a forceful sigh. 'That was the beginning. Curtis went to her, and she provided him with drugs. I remember how excited he was when he returned from the village. He claimed the old woman was a backwoods Pasteur. She had all manner of astounding potions, he said, and he wanted to study with her. I saw no harm in it, and told him to go ahead.

'It was about a month afterwards that Curtis ran out of heroin. Even with the *waidan*'s drugs to help him, it was a terrible ordeal. For a while I didn't think he would survive. Once the withdrawals had ended, he went through a period of several months during which he was sick both physically and mentally. Full of despair over his exile. Finally he began to improve, to get out, to walk, and eventually he restated his desire to work with the *waidan*. He asked if we could order some laboratory equipment. Bunsen burners, test tubes, a microscope, and so forth. I used some of your money to make the purchases. At first I was only humouring him. After all, he had no training in chemistry or biology, and I assumed his curiosity about herbal remedies would at best become a hobby. But he went about the work as if his life depended on it, and he

37

was so organized, so painstaking, I began to believe he might make some small contribution to the archaeology of medicine. Six months later, however, I realized that my assessment of his work had been well off the mark.

'The drug on which Curtis had been concentrating his studies is called *seribu aso*, which means "thousand dragons". It's a powerful hallucinogen that the Dayaks believe puts them in touch with the spirit world. Aside from its mystical application, it's used by the *waidans* to treat madness, their reasoning being that if a man can't be cured by ordinary means, his care should be given over to the spirits, who will drive out the devils. Curtis had been trying to develop a modified form of the drug. Both a modification and an enhancement. Why he was directed to this line of research, I don't know. I believe he was simply following the rule of his intuitions. In any case, one of the men who worked for me was stricken with a form of madness. He was disassociative. Screaming half the time. Violent. *Seribu aso* had been administered, but had done no good whatsoever, and the men had been forced to tie him up in one of the sheds. The missionary doctor at Long Selor was off somewhere, and I was at my wits' end. Then Curtis suggested that he administer his experimental drug. Naturally I refused to allow it, but one evening he dragged me down to the shed to see the madman. He'd bitten through his lower lip and, as I watched, he began to convulse. It was clear to me that he was dying and, while I had no great faith in Curtis's drug, I didn't believe it could make matters worse. I gave him permission to go ahead with it.'

Tenzer lifted a handful of loose photographs and let them sift through his fingers as if they were the ashes of some fond hope. 'He injected the man with the drug, and almost instantly the convulsions stopped. The man went rigid, his eyes staring. It was uncanny . . . that sudden cessation of sound and movement. I felt that the room had been invaded by a powerful presence, whose only sign was a pressure in the air. The rustling and cries from the jungle seemed to be registering the man's tension, and all his muscles were articulated. His skin glistened like wet mahogany in the lantern light. For fifteen or twenty minutes he lay motionless, and I was certain that the injection had brought him closer to death and not the reverse. And when at the end of that time he went limp, I believed that death had occurred. But a moment later he began to speak, not the delirious ravings of a madman, but prayerful mutterings. The pressure in the room was building, becoming so intense that my ears ached, and it appeared that mist was forming about the man's body. I thought I must be having a spell of some sort, but then I noticed Curtis holding his ears. I suppose I was afraid, yet I was so absorbed by what was happening that my fear was subsumed. The mist thickened. It looked as if a cocoon was being woven about the man. But the cocoon never fully materialized. Flickers of light began to emanate from the body, like tiny lightnings, and were transmitted along threads of the mist towards the head, coalescing there, forming a glowing oval that soon burst apart. For a fleeting instant, I saw something. . . . What, I cannot say for certain. It flew up out of the light and vanished. The image I retained was of a snarling face similar to the faces of the demons the Dayaks carve on their totems. With its exit, the pressure in my ears dwindled to nothing and the mist dissipated and the man lay quietly, his chest rising and falling with the rhythm of a deep sleep.

'A week later,' Tenzer went on, 'I wrote you an enthusiastic letter concerning Curtis. As I recall, it contained a number of overstatements relating to his abilities. But the man *had* been cured, and Curtis had come up with a theory that might well explain a large percentage of all mental illness. Stated simply, he believes that demons are responsible, and that he is in the process of developing a technique whereby they can be exorcized. Far-fetched it may be. However, I've seen it for myself. Curtis can justify the theory in quite a scholarly fashion. Unfortunately, there's much more to *seribu aso* – at least

to the drug Curtis has synthesized from it – than a cure
for demons.'

'Tell me about it,' I said.

'I don't know how I can,' said Tenzer wearily.

'Then why drag me in? If you don't know what the
problem is, why would you think I . . .?'

'Oh, I know what the problem is,' Tenzer said. 'Curtis
is the problem, and you, my friend, may be the solution.
You're the only person he respects, the only one who
ever helped him with no prospect of a return. Don't
forget that Curtis is an American, and where Kalimantan
is concerned, there are only two kinds of Americans.
Helpless children and violent children. Curtis has been
the first kind for most of his life, and now he's becoming
the second. He wants you here to approve of him . . . like
a proud father. And you *are* his father. The father of the
helpless child you sent into the jungle to find his strength.
He wants you to see how strong he's grown.'

'And what do *you* want?' I asked.

'I hope you can influence him,' he said. 'Persuade him
to stop taking the drug.'

'The same drug he gave the madman?'

'A variant. One much more powerful. He's taking
massive doses. He's spent months making it into something . . . something terrible.' Tenzer made a frustrated
gesture and then called out to his manservant. 'Irwan!
Whisky!'

A shadow came along the corridor, gradually taking
on form and colour as if re-entering the material world,
resolving into a withered Dayak in a batik sarong, with
rippling blue-black tattoos on his cheeks. He was bearing
a tray on which stood a decanter of whisky and two
glasses.

'Ask Irwan to explain things,' said Tenzer. 'His notions
make as much sense as any.'

As Irwan poured, I asked him his opinion of Mac-
Kinnon. Was he dangerous, more dangerous than other
men? *Not yet*, was the essence of Irwan's reply. And what

of the *waidan* of Tanjung Segar? Irwan said that she was not dead, that she had become part of MacKinnon's power. And what was this power? Irwan handed me a glass of whisky. 'The land,' he said. 'Curtis has spoken to the gods, he has awakened them, and they have answered.' He bowed and retired to the kitchen.

'Mystic gibberish,' said Tenzer. 'But I doubt there's a more acceptable explanation. If there is, Curtis will want to tell you.'

'Irwan claimed MacKinnon wasn't dangerous . . .'

'Not *yet* dangerous,' Tenzer corrected me. 'But I believe he's dangerous now. He wields a kind of power I can't fathom. He destroyed the radio to prevent me from summoning an investigator from the mission. He's hidden my guns. I'm afraid of him, and you should be, too. The Dayaks fear different things than we do. That they are not yet afraid should give you no comfort. And some *are* afraid – particularly those who have been long in the cities. Of course I don't expect you to heed me. You English are so damned bloody-minded.'

'First you slander the Americans, now the English,' I said testily.

'And why not? Your countries are responsible for the spilling of more innocent blood than any other. The greatest imperialist powers in history. Individually, you may be tolerable. But group you together or give you a little power, and you become childishly stupid and greedy.'

'Since you're passing out the national characteristics,' I said, 'let's hear about the Dutch.'

'We're an anonymous people,' he said. 'We have no qualities worthy of being stereotyped.'

'Except for the fact that you're slippery bastards.'

He raised his glass in a mocking toast. 'Perhaps more slippery than you know.'

'I've one further question,' I said. 'Three days ago I saw a man on a bridge near Tanjung Segar. Just at dawn. I couldn't see him clearly, but . . .'

41

'It was Curtis. He told me that morning he had seen you. How he manages this, I haven't the slightest.'

Irwan clattered things in the kitchen, giving me a start.

'The birds on the roof,' said Tenzer, 'they tell me when Curtis is near . . . even when he is far, far away.'

'Jesus God,' I said.

'The Dayaks tacked up the snakeskins and the flowers,' Tenzer said. 'But the birds and the butterflies, they simply appeared one day. They won't leave.'

Our eyes met across the desk, and I had the notion that an exchange took place along the channel of our linked stares, that some of Tenzer's wise fear flowed into me and was replaced in him by some of my ignorant vitality. The room seemed free of a tension that I noticed only by its sudden dispersion.

'Dinner won't be for several hours,' said Tenzer solemnly, as if this were the conclusion reached by our long conference. He hoisted his glass and examined the colour of the whisky in a slant of golden light. 'I imagine we could be very drunk by then.'

I was up before dawn the following morning, my head aching from the whisky, and I stood in front of Tenzer's house under a greying sky, wishing I had been more temperate. As the sky lightened, the birds atop the roof set up a squabbling, and the great trunks of the mahogany forest melted up from the darkness like the struts of a huge iron fence wreathed in mist. The sun edged up, visible through an avenue between the trunks, becoming a crimson fireball presiding over a tunnelled perspective of inky shadows and green glints.

I heard a cough and spotted MacKinnon standing by a corner piling of the house. He ambled over and, with what struck me as possessive pride, commented on the beauty of the sunrise. His hair was freshly washed, hanging in damp strands over his collar, and his smile, when he turned to me, seemed unnaturally beatific.

'I've been thinking about you for three years, Barnett,' he said. 'I figured I had a line on you, but it appears I may have exalted you a tad in my memory.'

'Always a mistake,' I said. 'Especially in this case. What I did for you was the product of a whim, nothing more.'

He nodded, regarding me soberly. 'C'mon,' he said. 'I'm going to give you a demonstration of something you won't believe.'

Beams of sanguine light lanced among the dark mahogany trunks as we walked, reddening a carpet of ferns and lichen-furred boulders. Birds in the canopy were making a chorus that sounded like the burbling of electric water; now and then a macacque shrilled out above them. It was that time of morning, always a brief moment in Kalimantan, when the air holds a certain freshness, and I came to feel revitalized, the pains of my hangover dissolving. My thoughts began to circulate with renewed vigour, and I had a stimulating awareness of where I was and in whose company – strolling through one of the last great wilderness with a man who might well have entered a new territory of the human mind. I wanted to believe that, you see. Despite Tenzer's warnings, I was excited for MacKinnon, hopeful for him, and I wondered then if that had been at the heart of my good deed four years before, if I had perceived in the wastrel the soul of an explorer. I was not sufficiently naive to accept this image of myself as spiritual talent scout, but the fact that I could even entertain such an idea was emblematic of my mood at the moment. Instead of being afraid, I was eager to know what he had discovered.

'You know,' he said as we crested a rise, 'it amazes me how so many men will try to deny that they've done someone a kindness.'

'If you're speaking about me,' I said, 'I'll admit I felt badly for you back in Banjormasim. But I'm neither a kindly nor a generous man. To be characterized as such, a man must be consistent in expressing those qualities. I certainly am not. If your comment has any bearing on human nature, it may be that when unkind men perform an act of kindness they tend to be ashamed, not because the act itself was wrong, but because they realize they can never live up to that standard.'

He laughed. 'You're no fool, whatever else you are. Of course I've known that ever since we met. I used to consider you a role model. Here's a man, I told myself, who's been dealing with these thieves for thirty years. Just look how he's made out.'

'But I wasn't dealing in drugs,' I said reprovingly.

'Don't get moral with me, Barnett. You've played in the shade yourself. Hell, I used to launder money through you.' He grinned at my surprise. 'I used Soedesarno as a middleman. I knew you'd be leery about working with me directly. The point is, though, you'd managed to cope with all the shit that was driving me crazy, and I respected you. That's why I came to you in the end. I wanted to ask your advice. But when I got to the shop, I felt like a fool. I couldn't bring myself to ask. Then you offered your help. Maybe it was a whim, maybe it was something else. It doesn't really matter now.'

He seemed determined to hold a high opinion of me, and I gave up trying to dissuade him. We passed beyond the mahogany trees into an area of the jungle dominated by secondary growth, where the canopy was less dense, the terrain broken, choked with bamboo and rotting trunks, some of which had fallen across the trail. Eventually we came to a clearing bounded by bamboo and saplings, centred by a slanting mass of grey stone embroidered with lichen and moss that burst from the earth like the prow of a sailing vessel petrified at the moment of its doom. MacKinnon took a seat atop it and pulled a small leather case from his hip pocket; within the case was a hypodermic needle and a vial of brackish-looking liquid. As he filled the hypodermic from the vial, I asked why – if all he'd had in mind was to give himself an injection – we had walked so far from the compound.

'This place,' he said, stripping off his belt. Then he chuckled. 'It's got antique vibrations.'

'Vibrations?' I scoffed at this.

'Yeah.' He cinched his belt around his arm, began pumping up a vein by opening and closing his fist. 'The drug works in concert with the old identities, the spirits . . . whatever you want to call 'em.' He glanced up at me. 'You may not believe me now, Barnett. But see how you feel in a bit.'

Once he had injected himself, he lay on his back, his eyes closed. A sweat broke on his forehead, and he began to shift about as if uncomfortable; shortly thereafter he grimaced, his face tightening, and let out a soft moan.

'Are you all right?' I asked, kneeling beside him.

'Don't talk to me,' he said, and groaned. 'I'm fine . . . Just leave me be.'

I moved away, sat cross-legged and watched the progress of his fever – that was, it appeared, the nature of what was happening to him. Sweat poured off him, and he twisted about. From time to time his eyes would snap open and he would stare fixedly at some object in the middle distance. Despite his assurances, I grew more and more concerned for him. It was getting hotter – a natural product of the ascending sun, I assumed; but soon I realized that the temperature was increasing with abnormal rapidity, as if the atmosphere itself had been infected with MacKinnon's fever. And perhaps it had, perhaps his symptoms had been transmitted throughout the air, for I began to feel ill myself, to experience disassociative impulses, odd thoughts rising from nowhere, words partnering in exotic combinations – much like the initial effects of a hallucinogen. Heat haze rippled from every surface, and this was especially pronounced near MacKinnon. I recalled how a mist had formed about the madman in Tenzer's story, and I thought the same thing might occur; but rather than thickening, the heat haze began to resolve into bright thready structures – thousands of glittering strings hanging in mid-air – that appeared to be flowing upwards yet remained in place, like light moving in splinters of mirrors. Before long, the clearing was thronged with these structures, and once they had achieved a dazzling brilliance, strong enough to cause me to squint, they flowed off into the jungle, the ground, the rock, vanishing in every direction. As a result everything within sight grew brighter, attaining an unearthly luminosity. Leaves sparkled, bamboo glowed like rods of gold, lichens glistened with the sheen of velvet. Even the motley greys of the stone acquired a dull shine redolent of platinum.

I was so entranced by this display that I had forgotten about MacKinnon, taking it for granted that he was either unconscious or incapable of speech. Thus I was startled when he sat up and – showing no sign of ill effects – told me to watch carefully.

'What should I watch?' I asked.

He only nodded and made a gesture that appeared to take in the entire surround.

Over the course of a minute or so, a pressure built in my ears. Once again I was reminded of Tenzer's story. But the pressure did not grow as intense as he had reported, reaching a level that, although painful, was not distracting. I couldn't hear a single noise, not a cry or a croak or a whisper of wind. Anxiety spidered the back of my neck. The silence was so extreme that, when I turned my head, I imagined I could hear the sinews twisting. Then I spotted a node of shadow among a cluster of leaves, differing from other shadows in that it began to spread, filling the separations of the leaves as if an invisible hand were inking in the empty spaces; those spaces left unfilled looked to be tunnels leading off through patchy sunlight and twitching bluish-green leaves. Within a minute or thereabouts, the clearing had been encaged by a blackness in which leaves and tree trunks and bamboo stalks were embedded, like vegetable litter buoyed up by tar, and when the blackness continued to spread, flowing upwards to stain the patch of sky above, I experienced an intense claustrophobic reaction and sank to my knees, expecting suffocation or worse. A few moments later, however, stars pricked the darkness, and I felt relieved – though no less disoriented. Embarrassed by my show of fear, I glanced at MacKinnon. Behind him, one of the trees bordering the clearing was glowing a supernal white. Every leaf and twig and articulation of bark was picked out in varying shades of white. Like a tree of bone. Perched on a low branch was a bird of some sort. A raptor, I decided, judging by its size and hooked beak. It, too, was white. It extended its wings and flapped towards me, moving slowly as would an object in a dream; instead of growing larger, it dwindled as it approached, until – although only a few feet away – it had shrunk to about the size of a dragonfly. More astonished than frightened by the apparition, I ducked and watched it soar up, then swoop towards Mackinnon. He did not try to avoid it, and it appeared to vanish into the dark oval of his head.

'MacKinnon?' I whispered.

He remained silent, motionless.

I kneeled beside him. Lodged at the centre of his left eye was a point of blazing white, and, before I could fall back or protect myself, it arrowed towards me – a diminutive hawk. Something cold penetrated my own left eye. It was not painful, only cold; yet I was terrified. I went rolling into the bamboo, shrieking and pawing at my face, wanting to tear out the thing, whatever it was. But as I thrashed about, I came to have a sense of amicable possession, to realize that the bird considered me a host equally suitable to the one it had just fled. This knowledge derived from its presence as naturally as steam rising from boiling water. I felt it perched like a white omen in the black ball of my pupil, and its quiescence, the precise quality of its stillness, was also a kind of knowledge. I understood that it was not entirely a spirit, that it was partly a production of the drug. The fact that this syncretic being had an affinity for me was somewhat reassuring, but the thought that it might shelter forever inside my eye caused a rekindling of my fear and I took to rubbing at the eye, shaking my head. The cold spot seemed to grow larger, and I imagined the bird assuming its original size within my eye, exploding the humour and swelling to fill the skull, pushing aside the brain tissue. I redoubled my efforts at ridding myself of the thing, giddy with fear, and I must have affected it somehow, for, as I pressed the heel of my hand against my eye, I felt the cold spot surge outwards and felt, too, a tearing pain in the flesh of my hand. Blood collected in the palm, webbing the seamed skin close to my wrist, and the realization that the thing in my eye had been of sufficient materiality to make the wound was so abhorrent, so threatening, that for the first time in my life I fainted.

When I recovered I found that the clearing had returned to normal. The sun was high, a humid breeze shifting the foliage, and MacKinnon was sitting close by, his face tight with what seemed a combination of eagerness and relief. He leaned over me and asked after my well-being. I told him that I was dizzy and cold, and that my hand hurt. I held it up to my eyes and saw that it had been wrapped in a piece of cloth torn from his shirt.

'It's not bad,' he said. 'Just a gouge.'

I had so many questions I wasn't able to frame even one, and before I could untangle my thoughts MacKinnon clapped his hands and said, 'Damn! I knew you'd be lucky for me.'

'Lucky!' I held out my injured hand. 'You call this lucky?'

'You don't understand,' he said. 'Some of my visualizations have produced tangible effects, but nothing pronounced. Just faint touches and ticklings, as if they were made of feathers or gauze. But this . . .' He gestured at my hand. 'I'm sorry you're hurt, but I've been waiting to see something like this for a long time.'

'Why?' I asked. 'Why is it so important that these . . . visualizations cause an effect?'

He seemed to be thinking over an answer, then gave

a diffident shrug and said, 'I suppose in the scheme of things it's not important at all. But I've worked on this for so long, I guess I want it to be really remarkable.'

'I wouldn't be concerned about that,' I said drily.

'I suppose not.' He laughed, and then leaned forward, intent upon me. 'Tell me what happened . . . how it felt.'

I related my experience with the white bird, but kept my relation minimal; I was growing more and more certain that he was untrustworthy, and I did not want to volunteer anything. Tenzer's assurance that nothing I saw could harm me had now been voided, and I viewed MacKinnon and his drug in a new and menacing light.

'Now,' I said when I had finished, 'suppose you give me your view of what's happening here.'

'How much did Tenzer tell you?'

I provided him with a summary of my conversation with Tenzer, and he nodded with amusement at several points.

'Actually,' he said, 'I can't tell you much more. Except that all along I've had the feeling that there was a progression involved, that either my control of the drug or my connection with the land – with the spirits, if you will – was growing stronger.'

'Oh, you can tell me quite a bit more,' I said. 'For instance, all the things I saw on my way here. Volcanoes, ghosts, and so forth. I assume they were some sort of spiritual manifestation. But if you weren't there, if you and the drug are the catalysts that cause the manifestations, then how—?'

'Places like this,' he said, waving off the remainder of my question, 'places where there's been spiritual activity in the past, once I've visited them, re-energized them, so to speak, they remain active for a while. And they become accessible to me in interesting ways as well.'

'Such as materializing at the centre of a suspension bridge?' I suggested.

'Yeah, like that,' he said. 'That stuff's weird. I don't even know it's going to happen most of the time. Then

49

suddenly I'll have a kind of doubled vision.' He spread his hands in a gesture of helplessness and grinned. 'That's all I know.'

'How did you know I was there?'

'I didn't, not really. But Tanjung Segar, all the other places . . . it's as if I'm sensitized to them. When something's happening in one of them, I'm drawn there.'

I absorbed this information, studying him. There seemed to be a new arrogance in his face, yet it struck me as being an affectation, and I had the idea that he was holding something back. I said as much, and after a pause he said, 'There's something else about all this . . . something disturbing. I'm not sure what it is, at least not sure enough to speculate. Maybe now with you here, I'll be inspired to look into it some more.'

'This other thing,' I asked, 'what do you think it is?'

He shook his head. 'Maybe I'll tell you in a day or two.'

'Don't you trust me?'

'Not with this,' he said. 'I wouldn't trust anyone with this. Not until I'm certain of what's going on.' Another dismal laugh. 'I tried to tell Tenzer about it back when I first started, and he accused me of being a madman. You'd probably think the same.'

We sat in silence a few moments, and then I asked him what he planned to do with all he had learned.

He appeared to be mulling the question over. 'Until now,' he said finally, 'I wasn't sure there was anything to do – except maybe to entertain in rather a spectacular way.'

'And now?'

He looked up at the white blur of the sun. 'What would *you* do?'

'I'd stay away from the drug,' I said. 'God knows how it's affecting your brain.'

'That's not important.'

'The hell you say! You may be killing yourself.'

He shrugged. 'I've been killing myself my entire life. At least this way it's for a reason.'

'But you're not sure what that reason might be.'

'Not yet . . . But I know there must be some right way to use all this, some good that can be done. Tenzer used to run on and on about the spirits, about how they protect the land. I've come to care for this place. Maybe I can do something to help protect it.' He gave me a searching look. 'C'mon, Barnett. If you were me, wouldn't you try to do something?'

No longer dizzy, I sat up, cradling my injured hand, and met his eyes. 'The first thing I'd do would be to ask myself if I was really in control. From what you've said, it's clear you're not at all certain about the nature of these events. You have a notion – and perhaps it's an accurate notion. Perhaps you are in league with the spirits. But even so, you don't seem to understand all the potentials involved. I wouldn't rush into anything if I were you. This needs a great deal more investigation than you've given it. You should offer the drug for testing by a qualified agency.'

I could see this displeased him. He got to his feet, paced to the edge of the clearing and stared out at the jungle. 'Sure,' he said. 'And have the whole thing swept under an official carpet.'

'That may be for the best,' I said.

'You sound like Tenzer.' He affected a sepulchral tone. 'There are some things men are not meant to know.'

'It's not that,' I said. 'But there *are* some things that not just anyone should know.'

He whirled on me, defiant. 'Are you saying I'm not responsible?'

'I'm merely suggesting— '

'What's it take to prove myself to you?' he said.

'I hardly think that's the point,' I said. 'The important thing is that you— '

'What the fuck do you know?' he shouted, his face darkening. He slammed a fist against his thigh. 'Goddamn it! I never should have brought you here!' He walked back towards me, glaring. 'You old fool! Just stay out of my way from now on!'

He spun about on his heels and, taking a swipe at a low-hanging branch, stalked off into the jungle.

MacKinnon's display of childish temper put the stamp of authority on a judgment that I had been hesitant to make – that he was not merely untrustworthy, but unbalanced. That same evening he apologized for his behaviour, explaining that he had been frustrated by my lack of enthusiasm, because he had so been hoping to impress me. From this and all else that had transpired, I realized that Tenzer's characterization of his feelings towards me as being that of a prodigal son towards a father was dead-on, and, drawing upon the experiences I'd had with my own father, I sought to manipulate MacKinnon by instilling guilt. I accepted his apology in a cold and distant fashion, making it plain that I had not forgiven him, adopting the role of a dignified old man who had been deeply offended. This, I believed, would not only cause him to be eager to please me, but would permit me more freedom; I doubted he would be zealous in keeping track of my movements once I let him know how little I cared for such scrutiny. And that would allow me the better to keep track of *his* movements.

I did not inform Tenzer of my plan. Truthfully, I had no plan, only an intent, that being to spy on MacKinnon, to make further judgments and – if action were required, if it were possible – to act. I hoped action would not be necessary. Despite everything, MacKinnon's resourcefulness in the face of his addiction seemed to me remarkable, and I was still quite in awe of his discovery, although I didn't understand it. At any rate, I rejected the tactic of enlisting Tenzer's aid. I doubted he would be able to hide his nervousness if I made him my complicitor, and I decided to associate myself with him in despair, to hold long conversations and wax morose over the future, thereby persuading MacKinnon that I was as harmless as his employer. Thus I spent long hours in Tenzer's study, indulging in gloomy and drunken discourse.

Though MacKinnon shared Tenzer's house, since their falling-out he had spent most nights in the outbuildings beyond the compound – two shacks on pilings and a hut with tarpaper walls – where the Dayaks who worked for Tenzer were quartered. Three days after my outing with MacKinnon in the jungle, I was standing by the compound gate at dusk, having a smoke, when he came out of the hut, shirtless and carrying a whisky bottle. I pretended not to notice him, keeping my eyes on the mahogany trees, on the grainy darkness into which they were fading, and slapped at a mosquito whining in my ear. I heard him approaching, felt him standing at my shoulder, but did not turn.

'How's it going?' he said.

'Quite well,' I said stiffly, and exhaled a plume of smoke that seemed to thicken the accumulating shadow.

'Look,' he said after a prickly silence. 'Can't we get past this?'

'According to you,' I said, 'I'm already past it.'

He let out a sigh of frustration. 'I'm tired of apologizing for that.'

'There's no need for apology,' I said. 'Soon I'll be out of your hair.'

'What do you mean?'

'Just that,' I said. 'I plan to spend a few more days with Paul and then head back to the coast.'

This was a trial balloon on my part. If he were planning a dangerous enterprise, I did not think he would permit me to leave. And also I wanted to learn how tolerant he would be of me.

'I wish you wouldn't,' he said.

'Why not?' I walked off a few paces and ground out my cigarette beneath my heel.

He followed me, eager as a hound. 'I really want your advice,' he said. 'I don't have anyone else to talk to about this.'

'I've already given you advice, and you've rejected it.'

'You haven't tried to see my point of view,' he said, petulance creeping into his voice. 'If you did . . .'

'I don't believe you have a point of view,' I said. 'When I look at you I see the most dangerous sort of person – a man with power and no moral agenda, just a diffuse notion that he should do good. It often takes an act of God to save us from do-gooders like you.'

'Do you actually believe I intend to hurt anyone?'

'Your intent,' I said, 'is irrelevant. Let me ask you a question. What element of your character should give me confidence that you have even the seeds of a capacity for right action? The fact that you're a reformed drug addict – or semi-reformed? You've obviously replaced heroin with something more volatile.'

'I'm not addicted,' he said. 'I— '

'Or should I look to your history with Pertamina? Should I take cognizance of how you've essentially imprisoned an old man who's done nothing but show you kindness? I'm not saying it's impossible for you to achieve something worthwhile, but, given your various failures of will and character, perhaps you'll understand why I'm dubious as to the quality of your moral fibre and the seriousness of your intent.'

It was apparent both during and following my outburst that he was struggling to control his temper, and that he was able to restrain himself from lashing out was a signal, I realized, of his willingness to accept such a rebuke in order to maintain the relationship. Whether or not his affection was healthy made no difference to my own intent. I was only interested in gauging the extent of my power over him.

'For the sake of argument,' he said, 'let's assume you're right about my moral incompetence. Doesn't that make it even more important that you help me, that you give me the benefit of your guidance?'

'You don't want help,' I said. 'You want approval.'

'That's not so.'

'Then tell me,' I said, 'where is the *maidan* of Tanjung Segar?'

I had been saving that question for just such a moment, hoping to catch him unawares during an emotional exchange, and in this I had succeeded. He made a perceptible attempt to master his expression, but I saw guilt in his face.

'Is that a difficult question?' I asked.

He turned away, had a drink from the bottle, scratched his beard. The soft chugging of the generator from within the compound seemed an organic sound – the engine responsible for the darkening of the air.

'It wasn't my fault,' said MacKinnon at last. He moved farther off, scuffing the grass, and when he looked back to me, for the first time I had a sense of his confusion, of his real need for help. Despite his beard and adult musculature, his hunched posture made him appear like a child expecting a beating. 'I suppose I should have known what would happen. Maybe I did know and refused to admit it.'

I waited for him to continue.

'She became jealous of me, of my relationship with the spirits,' he said. 'Like I told you, I should have expected that. But I had no idea she'd do what she did.'

'Which was?'

'She stole some of the drug. She didn't know how to give herself an injection, so she drank it – an entire vial. Several hundred doses.'

'She died?' I asked.

'You might think so,' he said defensively. 'But I don't. She's become part of the . . . the spiritual fabric. Whatever you want to call it.'

'That seems rather fanciful,' I said.

'Maybe it is, but you saw her. She appears all over the place, and I don't have anything to do with it. At least it doesn't feel like I do. The other stuff . . . I always feel it's me somehow, that I'm involved. But not with her.'

The subject obviously troubled him, whether because of guilt or the fact that the *waidan* was beyond his control. I decided to drop it. 'Has anyone else tried the drug?'

'No,' he said. 'And nobody's going to.'

'Of course,' I said. 'You wouldn't want to risk the usurpation of your power.' I laughed. 'Much like the *waidan*.'

Once again he struggled for control. 'That may be part of it,' he said. 'I'll admit it.'

'Could there be another reason?' I said. 'I mean, apart from your altruistic desire to bestow some indefinite blessing upon mankind.'

He fixed me with a resentful look, then strode off towards the hut; a moment later orange lantern light bloomed within. I lit another cigarette, leaned against the gate and considered the situation as the darkness became complete. In general, I was pleased by what had happened. Though I had my doubts as to MacKinnon's stability and intentions, I was certain that I had great leeway with him.

The next night at almost this same exact hour, I had once again stationed myself beside the gate for a smoke, when a young Dayak man and woman, both heavily tattooed and dressed in western clothing, came out of the compound and walked towards the jungle. As they passed MacKinnon's hut, he shouted and they stopped dead. He appeared in the doorway. I couldn't hear what was being said, but I could tell that the Dayak couple were upset. The man seemed by the tenor of his responses to be defying MacKinnon. I heard MacKinnon laugh. He stepped forward and lifted his arms like a priest supplicating the gods. The man drew back, and the woman dropped to her knees in front of MacKinnon as if begging for mercy. He lowered his arms and helped her to stand; he spoke sharply to the man, who hurried away. Then he pushed the woman ahead of him into the hut.

I thought I knew what had happened, that MacKinnon had used the threat of occult powers to force himself upon the woman, but to make certain I sneaked around the back of the hut and peeked through the window. MacKinnon was sitting on a pallet in the corner. He spoke to the woman in Dayak, telling her to hurry, and accompanied his command with a brusque gesture. She began to unbutton her dress. MacKinnon watched her, sipping from his bottle, his bearded face sweaty and brutish-looking in the unsteady light. Once the woman had finished undressing, he told her to get down on her hands and knees beside him. Her expression stoic, she obeyed. Posed on all fours, her breasts hanging down, staring at the lantern flame, with her dark tattoos and slim gleaming body, she appeared to be halfway through a transformation into the animal. I had expected MacKinnon would mount her immediately, but he remained seated, his head tipped back, and ran a hand along the woman's waist and flanks, the image of contented dissolution. I turned from the window, more distressed by this display than by anything I had previously witnessed. It was not his appropriation of the woman that disturbed me; it was what I had seen in his face – or rather what I had not seen. I no longer sensed in him an innocence, an untainted core. Power and drugs had eroded it. I imagined how his notion of protecting the land might manifest, a country patrolled by demons operating at his whim, and I knew now that Tenzer had been right – MacKinnon had to be stopped.

Throughout the first week of my stay at the trading post, Tenzer drank heavily. If he had been deteriorating prior to my arrival, then that deterioration was accelerating. He would lapse into senile reminiscences, long weepy rambles that were often punctuated by diatribes and bursts of profanity, all aimed at MacKinnon. In order to maintain my role of his companion in decline, I was forced to join him in bouts of drinking, though I tried to keep my intake of whisky at a minimum, and as we sat in his study late one afternoon, with a hard rain pounding the roof, he provided me with the key to a campaign against MacKinnon.

He had been talking about the old days, an evening when the two of us had watched a *waidan* perform a cure. 'That,' he said, 'now that was something truly wonderful, truly spiritual. Not like this.' He gazed out though the bamboo blinds. 'The land is being raped in a way I would never have thought possible. I expected loggers and all the rest. But this . . .' He sighed.

'You mean MacKinnon?' I asked.

'Of course I mean MacKinnon!' he said testily. 'Mac-Kinnon and his drugs and his stupid American heart!'

'I don't see what being American has to do with it,' I said.

'Then you're a damn fool!' Tenzer gave a stack of papers a feeble slap. 'Any common bastard can rip minerals out of the earth. It takes an American to violate the soul of a place.' He drained his glass of whisky. 'Usually it's their culture that's the weapon, but with MacKinnon it's his idiotic notion of morality. God only knows what sort of bizarre conversion he has in mind for us.'

'It seems to me,' I said, 'that although he's wielding the sword, the sword itself is the stuff of Kalimantan.'

In the rainy light that penetrated the blinds, Tenzer's face looked greyer and more haggard than usual; his hands moved as clumsily as crabs atop the litter on his desk. 'Only to a degree,' he said. 'You told me yourself than when that bird, whatever it was . . . when it dived into your eye, you perceived it as being syncretic. It's true that these damned hallucinations are the stuff of legend, but I believe that either the drug or MacKinnon himself has imbued them with a new character. He's changing them . . . changing the nature of the spirits.'

'That's a bit of an overstatement, isn't it?'

'I don't think so,' said Tenzer. 'Before Curtis became secretive about his work, he told me what he believed was happening. The old magics, the gods. They weren't being essentially changed. Their natures, their basic qualities, those things were left intact. But instead of ruling as they once had, they were being ruled. Their powers were functions of the drug. In effect, they were the tools of whoever acted to restore them. Imagine that! The spirits reduced to slaves. They need him in order to live again, and so they're bound to do his will.' He drummed his fingers on the desk. 'He tells me that he alone can achieve this mastery. However, I have the idea that the truth is quite the opposite.'

'What do you mean?'

'It's just— ' Tenzer appeared to be searching for the right words ' —I've had the feeling on occasion that he's not secure with any of this. And his possessiveness in relation to the drug leads me to believe that his is hardly an exclusive mastery. All this may be wishful thinking on my part. I can't confront him physically. I've tried to employ the natives against him but, although they're loyal to me, they're afraid of him. So what am I left with? The drug may be the only means of getting at him.'

'Then why haven't you investigated it?'

'He locks it up and sets a guard,' said Tenzer. 'I could deal with the lock, and I could lure the guard away from the house. But I'm too damned infirm to take advantage. It takes me ten minutes to climb the ladder to my own house. How much longer would it take if I was nervous? Besides, I'm not sure I could stand the physical stress of the drug.' He poured another drink and leaned back, propping the glass on his belly. 'All my suspicions may be delusions, anyway. I don't have any solid evidence. But I love this place, and I feel it's being threatened in a terrible way. I would do anything to save it, yet I can do nothing. And perhaps nothing can be done.'

We passed on to other topics, but that fragment of the conversation continued to gnaw at me, and after some deliberation I decided that I would attempt to steal some of the drug. I hadn't yet decided to take it, but I thought that, if I were to have it in my possession, it might make the decision more informed. Why I believed this . . . well, my reasoning escapes me. It may be that I had already made the decision and was trying to hide the fact, wanting to spare myself anxiety. I had a great respect for the drug, having seen its effects, and I wasn't eager to be under its influence. Yet at the same time I was attracted by the possibility of adventure. And further, if Tenzer was right and the drug could enable me to contend with MacKinnon, then I had no choice but to take it.

The drug was kept in a refrigerator in the second house within the compound. I had no doubt of my ability to deal with the lock, but I couldn't count on knowing MacKinnon's whereabouts at a given time. However, unable to contrive a means of guaranteeing his absence, I decided I would have to risk discovery, and so I watched and waited for a clear chance. My decision to act in this manner may seem precipitate, but the oppressive atmosphere at the trading post had persuaded me to employ desperate measures. And another factor entered in. Ten days passed, days during which MacKinnon's powers grew at an alarming rate. According to the Dayaks, the village of Lenawesin had been completely destroyed by a demon who had materialized from a cloud, and MacKinnon himself alluded in conversation to the fact that the process of materiality that had begun in the clearing had accelerated its evolution. At last I spotted him one sunny morning as he headed out into the jungle, the leather case containing the hypodermic tucked into his back pocket, and once I was certain he was gone, I hobbled up to the Dayak guard, pretending to have sprained my ankle, and begged him to fetch me a tool from the shack outside the compound, one that would take him several minutes to locate. My feigned injury made it apparent that I would be unable to negotiate the ladder that led up into the house, and thus the Dayak had no qualms about leaving his post. As soon as he was out of sight, I entered the house, carrying a vial containing coloured water that resembled the fluid with which MacKinnon had injected himself. I was nervous, but I had little trouble picking the lock. I removed a vial from a small rack within the refrigerator, replaced it with my vial and after locking it again, I took a hypodermic from among those lying on a table by the bed and hurried back to Tenzer's house.

My plan had been to hide the vial in Tenzer's refrigerator and wait for an opportunity to take it; but having the drug in hand was a temptation. From memory and MacKinnon's conversation, I knew I could approximate the correct dosage, and I had enough experience with drugs to understand and weigh the possible consequences. While my theft had been motivated by the notion that MacKinnon might pose a threat to me, to a world in which I had carved a comfortable niche, I had also become increasingly fascinated by the drug. It was not simply that I was attracted by the possibility of obtaining personal power. That, I admit, was a factor, though less of one at that juncture than a casual observer might have suspected. I had learned over the years to influence and ensnare, to confuse and misdirect, and power such as MacKinnon sought to control was not suited to my nature. The allure of the drug was complex, involving a desire akin to MacKinnon's youthful longings for the Orient and mystic lore, and also a wish to know, really to know, this unfathomable place that had drawn me and, at least in part, had come to own me. Holding up the vial to a shaft of light that penetrated the shutters of my bedroom, I imagined that I saw movement in its murky depths; that movement seemed the expression of palpable knowledge, of something I could touch and comprehend, and I decided that I should at the very least acquaint myself with the potentials of the drug.

I had considered returning to the clearing where MacKinnon had led me that first morning, since that was

61

the only place in which I could be sure of the 'vibrations'; but then I recalled the ruin of an old plantation house, the former seat of a rubber business, that lay closer at hand. It was, according to the locals, rife with spirits. Fearsome apparitions might await me there but, to avoid the fearful certainty of the white bird, I was willing to take the chance. The house was situated on a saddle between hills and overlooked a small valley that had once been choked with rubber plants. It was a large white house, two long storeys and a verandah, almost completely overgrown with creepers and epiphytes, with only patches of dilapidated white frame and tile roof showing through. The verandah was festooned with fungus and moss; plants sprouted from splits in the planking; through the vine-webbed wreckage of a door, I glimpsed sections of the interior, shadowy furniture, and further vegetable decay. There was the feeling of vibratory stillness and imminence that attaches to such ruins, but unlike the ruins to which archaeologists and tourists gravitate, this feeling had no attendant sense of the marvellous. It was depressing and moribund, with nothing to commend it to the sightseer, unless he had an appreciation for the grotesque.

I sat on the steps of the verandah, and after vacillating for a good long while between fear and temptation, I injected myself with a miniscule dose of the drug and lay back to wait for whatever would come. Almost immediately a sweat broke on my brow, my heart fluttered, and shortly thereafter my stomach began to cramp. But all this was distant from me, the pain occurring at a remove, as if afflicting some other person with whom I had a psychic connection. I recognized that I was in pain, noted that I was tossing about in reaction to the effects of the drug, but the greater portion of my mind was untroubled, preoccupied with the things I was coming to understand.

I had expected that my perceptions would be fragmented, and, indeed, for several minutes I was assaulted by so many impressions that this seemed the case; but I soon grew accustomed to the pace of the drug, to the rate at which these impressions were flowing to me, and rather than being overwhelmed, I was illuminated. These impressions had nothing in common with the flash visions and insights I'd previously associated with hallucinogens. Although my eyes were closed, I came to have an intimate knowledge of every object in the surround, every blade of grass and beetle, every leaf and grub and inch of bark. I felt their articulated shapes, the glimmers of their vitality, and the vital coherence with which they were conjoined. But of greater consequence, from these impressions I received a powerful understanding of the place, of Kalimantan itself – an understanding of far more depth than any I previously had. It was as if the veneer of ordinary sights and sounds and smells had been stripped away and a radiant core exposed, and I could feel not only the particularity of the land, its spiritual richness, but also the affinities with it that had developed over my years of residence, affinities that bound me in a web of attachment. It seemed now that this web was part and parcel of the unity I felt with the land, that it reflected the chemical make-up of the drug, which was in effect a map of Kalimantan – not of its actual terrain but, I believed, of its spiritual geography, of another country that overlaid and interfaced with the earth and the air, and that this congruence between the drug and the land and myself was something foreordained.

And yet everywhere I looked I realized that this was MacKinnon's place, not mine. His character rose like heat from the dark greenery, from the old ruin, the hill, and I decided that Tenzer must have been wrong in his opinion that someone else could master the drug. Something about MacKinnon, some factor of chemistry or spirit, I thought, must have allowed him to attain a special relationship with the drug and thus with the gods of Kalimantan. From those intimations of him, I realized that I had been too gentle in my judgment. I had not understood the extent of his corruption. Elements of the man he had been were still evident in his character – his affection for me, his hope that he could leave a mark – but these elements had come under the sway of a sense of manifest destiny, of his desire to be the agency of change in Kalimantan. Tenzer had been accurate in his assessment of the American character, of its brutal naivety, its conviction that it alone possesses the necessary moral stability and right-thinking perspective to decide the fate of those it considers backward. The Romans, I thought, must have held this same self-opinion during the early stages of their decline. And the British. But this was no instance of absolute power corrupting absolutely. That is too simple and benign a way of putting it, a means of camouflaging the will towards corruption that invests the human spirit. We are all small men and humble until time and circumstance shine a light upon our secret hollows and allow our arrogant and unfeeling natures to bloom.

These generalized insights were less alarming than my insights into MacKinnon's power over the land. If he were to learn of my usage of the drug, he would perceive me as a threat, and I doubted he would hesitate to kill me. And with his capacity for far-seeing, he might discover me at any moment. I came to my feet, unsteady from the drug, afraid that some horror would tear away the fabric of reality and leap towards me. No matter how fast I could run, if MacKinnon were to notice me, I was sure that he would be able to track me down. I couldn't think what to do. Then, attended by a chill that washed sluggishly down my spine like sleet crawling down a windowpane, I became aware of a presence behind me.

Convinced that MacKinnon, utilizing his arcane ability to be in two places at once, had materialized at the house, I whirled about, ready to plead for my life. But he was nowhere in sight. In his stead was the ghostly, transparent figure of an old Dayak woman in a filthy sarong, with filed teeth and snarled hair and a wrinkled, tattooed face: the face of the *waidan* of Tanjung Segar done as a faintly glowing sketch. I backed away, thinking she would attack;

64

but she made no move towards me, hovering a few inches off the ground, then lowering so that her feet disappeared beneath it, an apparition as wavering and insubstantial as a mirage, seeming at times to fold in upon herself. She stretched out a hand, a gesture of supplication, and to my amazement she spoke, calling me by name, and then saying in Dayak, in words so faint they might have been an artful fabrication of the wind, 'Help me.'

I was so startled by her capacity for speech that all my fear went glimmering. I stared for a moment, unsure how to respond, and finally said, 'I . . . uh . . . What do you want?'

'Help me,' she repeated. Her form rippled just as had the faces of the demons above her village, and her own face flattened, expanded, as if it were an oil slick spreading over the undulations of shallow water. I could see the house through her gauzy substance. Once again she pleaded for my help, and I asked again what I could do.

'*Seribu aso*,' she said, her voice louder, a dry sibilance.

'What about it?'

'The vial in your pocket,' she said. 'You must take it . . . all of it.'

'I'm not eager to die.'

With the constant distortions that affected her features, it was hard to read her expression, but it seemed that bewilderment registered on her face. 'You will not die.'

'Why should I be different from you?' I asked. 'My flesh is no stronger than yours.'

She drifted farther off, then back, and I sensed her consternation. 'What did Curtis' – she made the name into an epithet – 'tell you that he did to me?'

'Nothing,' I said. 'He told me you swallowed a vial of the drug, an overdose, and that you died as a result.'

She hissed. 'Curtis is very clever. With a single lie, he hides his crime and also hides from you the truth of *seribu aso*.'

'I don't understand,' I said.

65

'A small dose of the drug, such as the one you have taken, that is only the beginning of truth. To know everything, you must drink the contents of the vial. Then together we can defeat him.'

I was not convinced. 'If he's lying, then what *did* happen to you?'

'He did not completely lie,' she said. 'I took the drug without his knowledge – or so I believed. I could have defeated him myself, but before the drug could take full effect, while my body was still overwhelmed by its pains, someone murdered me.'

'Someone?' I said. 'Then you're not sure it was Mac-Kinnon?'

'I have many enemies,' she said. 'But Curtis is my great enemy.'

It struck me then that I was presuming to hold rational discourse with a ghost, and I questioned the credibility of my own witness. 'How can you be here?' I asked, and the *maidan*, her hair stirring in a wind that I could not feel, replied, 'The drug ensured my survival. It can sustain a soul torn loose from the flesh.' I started to speak, but she cut me off. 'Listen to me, Barnett. All men are fools, but you are a fool without teeth. Your only weapon is my guidance, so do not anger me with your doubts. I wish to destroy MacKinnon because of what he did to me. But it is you who will benefit most from his death. If Curtis learns you have taken the drug – and sooner or later he will – he'll kill you. You must know that. Your only hope is to do as I say.'

I hesitated, and she gave a hiss that signalled her impatience. 'Take the drug, Barnett. Then you will enter the world that MacKinnon truly seeks to rule. Then you will understand in full why he must die.'

'I can't,' I said.

'Are you afraid?' she asked. 'Good. Fear is useful, and you will need fear to survive. The ghosts you have seen, the fires in the earth, the musics falling from the air – these arise from the forced conjunction of this world and another that adjoins it. They are like the sparks struck from the smashing together of two pieces of metal. You must enter that other world and there you can contend with Curtis. Here you are no match for him.'

'You mean the spirit world?' I asked.

She made a noise of disgust. 'There are no spirits, Barnett. Not such as you imagine them. There are no gods. There never were, there never will be . . . not unless MacKinnon succeeds in making himself a god.'

'But what are you,' I asked, 'if not a spirit?'

'Answer me this, Barnett. If you had no word for what you are, no term, how then would you describe your being? I do not know what to call myself. Perhaps I am a spirit. But I am something new, something that has never been before. I have nothing in common with those things that Curtis calls spirits. They and all that you have seen are no more than what I have said. Images trapped between the worlds, vague presences left from previous and more natural conjunctions that Curtis's drug enlivens.'

'Then he didn't lie about that,' I said.

'He does not understand,' she said. 'He still believes in the spirits, but what he controls is illusion. Granted, it is an illusion so powerful that it can destroy.'

'And heal?' I said. 'What about the man he cured?'

'Yes,' she said. 'He also has that power. But do you believe he will limit himself to healing?'

I continued to question her, and after a considerable time, after much clarification of terms, I put together a picture of what she was trying to tell me. The things I'd seen were spirits only in the most marginal sense; they were images trapped in a limbo between the worlds, and these images were stimulated by MacKinnon's drug. That he could use them to injure and heal she attributed to the drug's effect on the centre of psychic powers within the brain. She was vague about this, but as I understood it *seribu aso* had been used not to cast out devils, but to project the force of the *waidans*' personalities and create in the mind of the patient the confidence that he or she was being healed: a hallucinogenic cross between positive-thinking and bio-feedback. 'Devils' was simply a convenient term with which the *waidans* referred to the causes of disease. They believed, like a growing number of western doctors, that while many diseases could be traced to germs and viruses and so forth, there were other, deeper causes of ill health, and some of these were due to subtle mental instabilities. Despite its capacity for misuse, Curtis's drug, with its ability to give an illusory materiality to these causes, was a powerful healing tool. Even the wound on my hand, the *waidan* claimed, had been brought about by my conviction that it could be made, assisted by the force of MacKinnon's personality. But there was another side to *seribu aso*. The *waidans* used it to see into a world that they claimed interfaced with ours. When I asked the *waidan* if she was talking about an alternate universe, she failed to understand me and insisted that it was merely another world, one with its own laws and constants. They had a protective attitude toward this world, considering it a place of relative innocence, and she seemed more concerned with its fate than with that of Kalimantan. Curtis's drug allowed him actually to enter that world, but he was afraid of it and thus far he had done no more than investigate its borders.

The *waidan* was, to my mind, being deliberately vague about this other world, and I began to believe that she was lying, that her tale was designed to hide a more dire reality. But then, after more questions, she told me something that, although hardly solid evidence, gave it a little more credence.

'Long ago,' she said, 'the Punan Dayak went beyond the borders, and it is there they now live – there in the world they had travelled only in their dreams. You must cross the border too.'

'How could they cross over?' I asked. 'They didn't have Curtis's drug.'

'They were always bound there,' she said. 'For a thousand generations they trekked through the jungle searching for it, dreaming of it, drawn by its beauty. They became a people of dreams, and eventually, one by one, they reached their dreamed-of destination.'

I kept on questioning her, hoping for a clearer explanation, but she became impatient.

'You must cross the border,' she said again. 'Curtis will know and he will follow. He will fear that you'll learn some secret that will give you more power than he. Since the death of my body, I have come to know that land and its secrets. I will guide you and be your ally. Together we will kill him.' She drifted nearer, her face so close to mine that I made out the translucent structures of her eyes – the ghosts of eyes, yet they communicated her rage and desperation. 'His power is growing. You have to act now, while there is still time!'

'I need to think,' I said. 'I don't know what to believe any more.'

'Believe this. If you do not act soon, you will be a dead man.' She drifted back towards the ruined doorway. 'Tomorrow,' she said, 'I will wait here for you. Bring more of the drug. You may have a long journey ahead, and you cannot risk returning before your task is completed. If you are not here tomorrow, it may be too late. Day by day, Curtis is becoming more bold, more likely to cross over and learn the secrets of the world beyond.'

'What are they?' I asked. 'What sort of secrets?'

'Tomorrow,' she said, passing back inside the house, becoming a wraith against the shadowy background. 'Tomorrow.'

That evening I remembered what MacKinnon had once said, that he had confided early on in Tenzer about his knowledge of the thing that he had refrained from telling me. Despite her convincing performance, I wasn't certain that I trusted the *waidan*, and I hoped that, by questioning Tenzer, I might either corroborate or debunk her story of that alternate world. When I entered his study, however, I found him to be in worse shape than ever and thus a much less than credible witness.

It was raining again, the air thick and damp, and he was sitting at his desk, his hands moving in a pool of lamplight, trembling like old brown animals, lifting one after another of his photographs. Shots of jungle cats, orang-utans, the entire variety of Kalimantan's fauna. Now and again he would hold one of the photographs close to his face and trace the outlines of the subject with a palsied finger, as if trying to conjure it to life. I sat down opposite him, poured a glass of whisky from his decanter and waited for him to acknowledge me.

'Beautiful,' he said after a moment, caressing the photograph of a spectral tarsier. 'They were so beautiful.'

'*Were?*' I said. 'Aren't you putting them under the ground a bit prematurely?'

He blinked, his rheumy left eye leaking a tear; he seemed not to recognize me and lowered his gaze once again to the photograph.

I asked how he was feeling, and he merely waved at me without looking up, as if to indicate that the topic was of little consequence. I sipped my whisky, listened to the steady drumming of the rain. MacKinnon had not returned from his foray into the jungle – perhaps he was even now wandering that strange place beyond the borders of the world – and for that I was grateful; but even were I to convince myself of that other world's existence, I did not know if I would have the courage of my convictions. I considered giving up on the matter, retreating to the safe harbour of my shop. No matter what excesses MacKinnon might commit, I would likely be able to live out the remainder of my life in peace. What good reason, I asked myself, was there to risk those remaining peaceful days? I could find no answer to that question other than the most vague altruism, a motivation at which I had long been prone to scoff. Yet I was unable now to dismiss it out of hand, and, after pouring another whisky, I began to press Tenzer for information about MacKinnon.

At first he would only rail against him, loosing a stream of curses, then offering further dissections of his character. 'The man's a slug with a brain,' he said. 'All his life he's been lazy, sedentary. The only thing that's ever provoked him to move has been a drug of one sort or another. And when he does move, he can't help but leave a slimy track. I suppose we should pity him.'

'That's all well and good,' I said, 'but it's not very helpful.'

'Oh!' He gave a sodden laugh, wiped spittle from his chin. 'You want me to be helpful.' His eyes rolled up to the ceiling. 'God!' he said, fingering his photographs. 'God, I . . .' His head lolled onto his chest, and he muttered something unintelligible. Beyond him, the lamplit slants of rain in the blackness seemed a radiant sleet that threatened to break through the glass and hasten his dissolution. He picked up another photograph, that of an egret, and stared at it; his Adam's apple bobbed, his eyes glistened. 'I'd give anything . . .' he said, and let the words hang.

I continued pressing him and at last, after nearly an hour, managed to elicit a communicative response. 'He told me something once . . . I don't know,' said Tenzer. 'This place he'd found in the jungle. A beautiful place . . . strange. A place only the Punan Dayak knew. I can't remember. He told me so much. Gibberish, madness. Drug talk. And lies! Mostly it was lies.' He fell back in his chair. 'What does it matter, Barnett? It's over.'

'This place,' I said, 'did he tell you where it was?'

'Oh, he told me everything about it,' Tenzer said. 'Everything. And, God help me, I wanted to believe him. It was so beautiful! An Eden, a lost Eden!' He let out a sob and made a feeble gesture of dismissal. 'Let him take us all to hell! We're bound there anyway.'

I was astonished by the extent of his slippage, and I felt helpless in the face of such a profound failure; but nonetheless I mumbled that maybe something could be done, hoping to boost his spirits. He only laughed.

'You never fail to amaze me, Barnett. Always the master of the situation. Who do you think you are – God? You're just an aging swindler who's managed to attain' – he hiccupped – 'a measure of respectability. But you can't win this fight by swindling, by cheating. I never should have asked you to leave your little nest. You're out of your element here. This situation calls for a man, not a petty crook.'

I didn't dispute his characterization of me. I might have, had he not been so pathetic; but even if I had disputed it, in my heart I knew it was more-or-less accurate. I sat staring into my whisky glass, half-listening to him babble, to the rain, to the morose rattle of my thoughts, and it was not until sometime later that I realized Tenzer was praying, begging the Lord to lift his burden and comfort his afflictions, to bestow upon him the peace that passeth all understanding. I was horrified. Tenzer was a private man, and this ultimate revelation of inner frailty – so it seemed to me – brought home the finality of his plight. With his head thrown back, withered neck exposed to the cutting edge of the divine, his eyes closed and streaming tears, he implored the Creator to stop his brain this very moment. He looked to be straining upwards, like a diver poised before making an arcing leap.

I wanted to leave the room, but the sound of his words and the sight of his pitiful aspect pinned me to my chair, leaving me helpless, harrowed by all I saw and heard. What worth did caution have, I asked myself, when it led to this? I would grow older and older, and end, like Tenzer, in a gush of feeble prayer and rotten thought. I was more afraid of that scenario than I had ever been of man or beast; I could feel the fraying of my flesh, my mind, my soul guttering like a candle stub, and it was at that moment, determined to avoid such an inglorious fate, that I decided to heed the *waidan*'s advice.

*

72

The next morning, sitting on the verandah steps of the ruined plantation house, I drank an entire vial of MacKinnon's drug. I had two more vials in the breast pocket of my shirt, having persuaded the guard to run another meaningless errand on the previous evening, and I carried a pack containing a sleeping bag, a torch, dried food, and so forth. I was as confident as one could expect under the circumstances. That MacKinnon had told Tenzer of a beautiful lost world seemed to validate what the *maidan* had said, and in truth I could not think of a reason why she would lie to me . . . unless her experience with MacKinnon had instilled in her a hatred of all foreign devils. But as she floated before me, the shafts of sun making a curious play with her gauzy substance, bringing to light odd internal structures like the fracture planes in a fragment of crystal, she gave no sign of hating me. Instead, she was solicitous, asking how I felt, and when I replied that I had some discomfort, stomach cramps, fever, she told me that I need not be concerned if these symptoms intensified, and that I might well lose consciousness.

'Wonderful,' I said, gritting my teeth against a particularly violent spasm, beginning to doubt my decision anew and also to marvel once again at the unreality of our dialogue. 'Tell me some more about this place we're going to.'

'You'll see it soon enough,' was her reply.

'It would take my mind off things to talk,' I said.

She shrugged. 'There's a deserted city near a river,' she said.

'A city? You mean a village?'

'No, a city. Not Dayak. You see, that world too has been colonized, though not by the English or Dutch. There are no Dutchmen or Englishmen there.'

She said this last with a relish that I found annoying. Sweat was pouring off me, and I was in no mood to play games. 'For God 's sake,' I said, 'do I have to drag every bit of information out of you? Whose city is it?'

'The builders have been gone for many centuries,' she said. 'The Punan Dayak say they came from the sky, that they lived in the sky. At least this is what they have dreamed.'

A cramp doubled me up, drawing forth a gasp.

'The city is a strange place,' the *waidan* continued in a disinterested tone, as if she were relating some obvious truth to a child. 'Very strange. Not at all like Banjormasim or the cities of the coast. I think we will be able to use it against Curtis.'

'I don't understand,' I said, flopping onto my back, half-blinded by the sun. I was dizzy, and my vision was playing tricks: there seemed to be a tunnel connecting me with every object in the landscape, a tunnel that had the shape of each particular object, and, whenever I looked at anything, I had the sense that they were swooping towards me and looming large . . . or else I would feel that I was growing very, very small.

'The city is its own power,' she said, 'and has nothing to do with *seribu aso*. It is immune to Curtis's control, and there are pitfalls he may not be able to foresee. I have explored it, and I have seen devices that may be weapons. I would use them against him myself, but' – she examined the palms of her hands – 'I cannot even touch them.'

'What sort of weapons?' I asked.

'You will see.' She drifted closer to me, her tattooed face appearing for a moment to bloat and distort. 'In the jungle, Curtis would kill you easily. In the city, he may still have the advantage over you because he controls his illusions. But we will have been there for at least a day before he can reach us, and this will enable us to gain our own advantage.'

'Why . . .?' Once again I was immobilized by a cramp. 'Why didn't you say anything about this before?'

'I wanted to find out what sort of man you were, Barnett,' she said.

'From your obvious disdain,' I said, 'I've assumed you already knew all you needed to know about me.'

74

'Perhaps so,' she said. 'But I wanted to learn whether or not you had the courage to face Curtis without knowing how you would fight him.'

'Courage!' I essayed a laugh, but it had more the sound of a racking cough; I was growing dizzier, and my vision was failing. 'That's scarcely what's motivating me!'

'What does motivate you then?' she asked.

I could have told her it was fear and desperation that drove me, and she would have gleaned from that some rudimentary conception of my motives. However, at that moment I had an overwhelming sense of the mystery that we posed to one another. She could never understand the complex of greed and love and fear and revulsion that not only motivated me in this instance, but underwrote so many of my actions. And I realized that this stew of compulsions comprised a motivational essence for someone of my age and experience, and that the *waidan* would have much more difficulty comprehending something so fundamentally Western than she would the underpinnings of a superficial quality or habit. The superficial was what we perceived most about the other. Disembodied, a mere sliver of a thing, she was clearer to me than she would ever have been in the flesh. It was easier for me to discern her cultural idiosyncrasies in that phantom form, to be aware of the strangeness that had informed both her life and this peculiar afterlife, because over the past weeks I had been conditioned to strangeness. I could no longer take her for granted or dismiss her out of hand. She was a witch, a woman of the forests, a seer into other worlds, and in many ways I was a child beside her. Yet despite our differences, we shared one compulsion, no matter how refined it might be in her case or how impure in mine: a reverence for the land, for the wilds of Kalimantan. And watching her drift and change, I was born again into that reverent state, lifted from the pain of my body into the contemplative. The play of light along the internal structures of her body began to seem a vast

75

panorama – it was as if I were looking out onto a place of quartz cliffs struck by immense beams of sun, the sort that shine down through breaks in an overcast sky, articulated by droplets of moisture. Shimmering, alien light. The cliffs were alive with prisms; spills of silver water broke thousands of feet below into the shadow of the jungle. It was like no place I had ever seen, but nonetheless I believed it to be some unexplored and uncorrupted corner of Kalimantan. It had that familiar dark green stench of mingled decay and freshness, a stink of life that rose from the lowlands to those shining heights, combining there with stinging ozones, and I became entranced by the scent, by the prisms, the waterfalls, by every element of the scene, drawn towards it as towards a hypnotist's spinning jewel. I was fading into that place, I thought, tunnelling towards it, all else dimming, darkening, becoming a black frame for a bright distance. Pain lay somewhere far behind me, a blazing country ago, and in its stead I began to feel a translucent brightness, as if I had cast off a shroud of flesh and bone, as if my essential things had been freed and were growing radiant, delicately shifting, transformed into ghostly structures that in their otherworldly intensity were the equal of the *waidan*'s eyes.

I had expected, when I awoke, to find myself upon those crystal cliffs, believing that they were an actual landmark; but the chief distinctions between where I had been sitting and the small clearing where I now lay were the absence of the plantation house and the density of the surrounding jungle, and I wondered if somehow the *waidan* – who was nowhere to be seen – had played a trick on me and I was still a short walk from Tenzer's trading post. Yet on coming to my feet and casting about for her, I began to notice other distinctions. For one, the sounds of the jungle had changed. The cries of birds and the shrillings of insects were unfamiliar in their pitches and cadences, and not once did I hear a monkey chattering. And the smell, though pungent and decaying, was not

76

precisely the same as it had been. It was cooler by, I estimated, about ten degrees. The sun was not quite right, and the sky was brushed with a faint violet hue. Once I had noticed them, these changes bore in upon me, and I began to tremble, afraid as never before. To an extent, the fear attendant upon the prospect of travelling beyond the ends of the earth had been glossed over both by despair and a resurgence of my youthful desire for adventure; but though my mind may have reached an accommodation with the risks involved, my body had not, and it seemed now that my component cells were experiencing a basic fear, pumping out the chemicals of desperation. The notion that the *waidan* had abandoned me tuned my fear several notches higher, and without a thought for caution, with no clear idea of what I might accomplish, I went crashing through the brush, plunging into a dark, densely canopied stretch of terrain, stirring up winged things, the racket of my passage causing the dwellers in the canopy to scream and hoot. A few minutes later I realized that if the *waidan* had inadvertently become separated from me during transit, she might have known my exact destination and would search for me at the spot where I had found myself lying. But when I stopped and glanced about, intending to return to the clearing, I discovered that I was lost. Sunbeams as distinct and thin as lasers punched down through the leaves, illuminating tiny patches of soil, like a scattering of glowing golden coins. I could see little other than the sinister shapes of ferns and the shadowy trunks of the nearby trees.

The urge to surrender to my panic was extreme, but I managed to subdue it and set about trying to locate the clearing. After backtracking for approximately five minutes, I spotted an area of brightness off to my right and believed that I had succeeded in retracing my steps. Soon, however, it became apparent that I had gone astray. It was no small clearing ahead. Sunlight showed between the trunks for a space of at least two hundred feet, and, as I drew closer, I made out a wide expanse of murky green

77

water with marshlands on the opposite bank. Recalling what the *maidan* had said about a city lying near a river gave me heart, and I hurried forward. But when I came out from beneath the canopy, pushing through a fringe of bushes with spiky leaves, what I saw rekindled my fear and rooted me to the spot.

Banjormasim was still enough of a backwater so that reading materials in English were difficult to obtain, and over the years, in order to satisfy an expatriate yearning for printed matter in my mother tongue, I had been forced to read whatever came to hand: magazines concerned with factory management and horticulture, astronomy texts, guide books, manuals on how to play bridge and home improvements and automobile repair, paperback novels by the hundreds, among them a number of science fiction works. The covers of these last sometimes featured images of wrecked spaceships – vast hulks with charred rocket tubes, holed by meteors or blown nearly in half by blasts of energy, encumbered by vines, home to a variety of exotic fauna. However, my nodding acquaintance with speculative fiction had not prepared me for the wreck that lay mired in the rank grasses on the far side of the river. In many respects it conformed to the images adorning the covers of those paperbacks. Saucer-shaped; fashioned of mirror-bright metal; warty opaque blisters ringing the uppermost portion; enormous – by my reckoning, it was at least half a mile in diameter. It was wedged into the marsh at an angle like that of a discus stuck in the mud so as to reveal a gaping hole in its underbelly, and in its shadow, secret things darted and wriggled. But while those artists' renderings had been desolate and dead, redolent of ancient deserted castles, there was about this wreck an atmosphere of kinetic frenzy. Webs of bluish-white lightnings crawled and crackled across the metal skin, spreading to encage the entire upper portion, then ebbing so that an inconstant glow was just visible along the rim of the thing, alternating between these states at random intervals; straining my ears, I could hear a crackling noise above the slop of the river. Lashing out from the hole – hole, I say, but it would be more accurate to describe it as a cavern, for the entrance was as big as the door of an aeroplane hangar – were dozens of segmented grey tentacles, each appearing to be more than a hundred feet in length. Initially I assumed them to be flesh, the appendages of some animal sheltering within, but after observing their operations and watching the sun dazzle off their joints, I understood that they must be made of metal or plastic or some other inorganic material. Some were tipped with bulges of crystal, and from the crystals spat pale red beams that flickered and were extinguished in the air; others coiled and bent inwards like concerned serpents toward the ragged edges of the cavity, and from their nozzled tips there spread a haze of dark particles, like a floating pollen of graphite. Occasionally one of the crystal-tipped tentacles would emit a beam that coincided with a portion of the haze and for a moment – the length of time it took before the tentacle lashed away and fired its beam in another direction – the haze would appear to solidify. I decided that the actions of the tentacles must be designed to repair the damage and that they too were in need of repair. From time to time, flocks of whirling prisms, like the souls of birds, would pour from the shadowy guts of the ship and circle above it, dissipating one by one; and every fifteen minutes something large would go rippling away from the ship through the grasses, hidden from view, perhaps travelling beneath the water, throwing up gouts of mud and steam as might the mad, monstrous child of some burrowing creature. A form of exhaust, I thought; a discharge of some kind. And the opaque blisters of the ports – so I thought of them – they were also in motion, some bulging upwards, some shifting about, some dimpling inwards, some vanishing and leaving a flat smooth expanse of metal in their stead: it appeared that they were the expressions of a fluid force that, like blood, pervaded the skin of the ship and imposed structural change.

All this chaotic turbulence fostered the impression that the wreck had occurred recently, yet it had an aura of tremendous age, and I came to believe that I was witnessing the result of a disaster that had happened millennia before; that the tentacles and webs of energy and all the rest were the twitches of a mortally wounded organism, one that had taken ten thousand years thus far to die and would take ten thousand more to grow completely inert, its machine heart sputtering and failing under an alien star. Framed by the marsh and the river and that oddly hued sky, with another section of jungle in the distance and birds wheeling overhead, it was an utterly compelling sight. I was spellbound, so thoroughly distracted that for a long moment I forgot to draw breath. And when at last I reawakened to my circumstance and told myself that I had best push on, I remained captivated. I wanted to stay until I had branded the image onto my eyes, memorized every detail. Here, it seemed, was the essence of the mystery I had always sensed at the heart of Kalimantan, and like a pilgrim who after years of unrewarded searching had glimpsed the transcendent object of his faith, I was reluctant to put it behind me. God, the size of the thing! It was large enough, I felt, to inspire its own moral sphere. Gravity must flow around it, light must become solid in its vicinity. It was not beautiful, not ugly, neither sad nor evil. It was only itself, a presence that defied labels or comparatives. And I could not have been more dumbstruck had the clouds opened and Jesus come riding down on a shaft of glory. Life had finally and unexpectedly measured up to my childlike hopes for it.

Eventually, moved by the gathering twilight to address the problem of survival, I started walking along the bank – camping beside the wreck would have proved too unsettling. Obeying my instincts, I followed the path of the declining sun, looking for a sheltered place, a little cove perhaps, where I might feel secure. Within a matter of minutes, I rounded a bend and lost sight of the wreck, and after half an hour or thereabouts I found a spot where the jungle closed in on both sides of the river, and the bank sloped down to a gravelly shingle, bordered by sheer rock faces some twenty or twenty-five feet in height. By the time darkness fell, I was as cosy as the circumstances permitted, sitting cross-legged on my sleeping bag, with a nice fire going and my belly full of jerky, bread, and dried fruit. The presence of mosquitoes comforted me by their familiarity, and I was happy to have to apply repellent. It was windless, but the heat was not severe; in fact, there came to be a touch of damp chill in the air. The fire snapped, water gulped against the rock, and from the jungle issued the noises of frogs and insects and night birds, noises – as I have stated – a shade different from those of home, but similar enough to complement my feeling of untroubled solitude. I could almost believe that I was back in the jungle near Tenzer's compound. The stars, however, put the lie to that. Like the stars of Borneo, they were myriad and bright, their radiance transforming the river into a shimmering dark jade coil, but they were so densely arrayed that I was hard pressed to discover any patterns among them. There was no sign of the Southern Cross or any of the usual constellations. To stave off anxiety, I made a game of illuminating the black page of the sky with starry tigers and water buffalo and sailing ships. I stared at the stars for such a long while that when I began see other lights in the sky, I thought I must have overstrained my eyes; but soon these new lights acquired added definition, as if fading in from another dimension, and obscured the stars, and I realized that they were actual, a phenomenon peculiar to the place: an intricate latticework of light that spanned a third of the sky, reminding me of those congregations of bioluminescent jellyfish that sometimes appear on the surface of the night sea, fading and brightening like living lace, like immense snowflakes drifting on the swells. There were patterns aplenty in this brilliant configuration. I could see anything I wanted there – faces, mystic symbols, batik designs, anything at all. It was as compelling a sight as the wrecked ship had been, but a less dominating one, its alienness outmatched by its beauty; and rather than enforcing a sense of displacement, it imbued me with calm, allowing me to go past my anxieties and recognize what the Punan Dayak must have recognized – that this world was sweet and new and unbroken, that spoilage here was a natural process and not the outcome of billion-dollar swindles and moral decay, and that though there might be dangers, beasts and serpents and worse, there were no dangers to the soul. Here one could breathe untainted air and, free from the confusion of business, the howl of life insurance, and the snaky kiss of greed, could gain a perspective that would let one know oneself and thus the world. I wanted it, I wanted to stay, to live and know these things. But I was there only by sufferance, bearing a chemical visa that permitted me – what? A few days. No more than that, I suspected. Yet not even this thought could oppress me, nor could the gradual dispersion of the lights in the sky diminish my clarity and calm. I could always return, I told myself. I would bring a few select friends to witness this pristine glory. I would become the official guide and administrator of Eden.

Not long after the lights had vanished, I spotted turbulence in the river, a roiling at mid-stream, and a moment later something surfaced – or did so partially – exposing a length of glistening dark skin that looked to be as thick as a mahogany trunk. The water continued to churn and billow upwards as the creature passed, a passage that lasted for at least ten seconds, and, taking into account the rate at which it travelled, I estimated that it must have been over a hundred feet long. Once it had gone, though I gave some thought to retreating into the jungle, I realized that I had been unafraid, convinced that the creature was not at all interested in me. This was a dangerous precedent, to depend on this sort of feeling, but nevertheless I trusted it, and I wondered if I might not be more in touch with my sixth sense than I'd been at home. Given all that had happened, I felt amazingly clear-headed, and when I examined the confidence I'd had in my choice of campsite, I found that it had been unnaturally sure. Perhaps this was illusory, but I was not quite able to believe that. Something in the magnetic field sensitizing the brain? Something in the atmosphere? Who could say? Those kinds of answers had never been important to me, at any rate. It was the discovery, the challenge and the allure of the new that had always commanded me. There was an innate comprehension possible in an active life that provided a man with more than enough to ponder and sustain him. Science was a fool, history a swindler, psychology a stick adorned with bones and feathers, and analysis was best left to those who for one reason or another had disengaged from life. Thinking this was not, as one might suspect, an act fraught with pomposity. It had, as did all my thoughts then, the ring of common truth. It was something that I knew, that was true for me, and I had no urge to broadcast it, to compare its virtues or make it true for anyone else.

Despite the tenuousness of my situation, I had not felt so at peace in years. This was due partly to the beauty and wildness of the river, but I believe it was more a product of a change in my internal geography. How long, I wondered, had it been since I had done anything for the pure sake of doing it? Oh, there were other factors involved, to be sure, yet that was at the root of why I had left the relative security of Tenzer's compound. I might have persuaded MacKinnon of my harmlessness, I might have been able to manipulate him. But I had needed to act once again with the casual recklessness of youth, to follow my heart, not my head, and that was in essence what I had done. And having done so, I had been liberated from the web of petty concerns with which I had become fettered in Banjormasim. Liberation of this sort, I knew, had its price, yet I was prepared to pay it, fully aware of the penalties that might accrue.

I settled back on the sleeping bag, drowsing, and soon I came to see myself as if from a height, a tiny figure stretched out on the sand, with the fire a reddish-orange spearpoint twisting up into smoke ghosts that turned a luminous blue and attenuated into wisps against the night sky and the ragged wall of the jungle. There was a light around me, a pearly shell of cool sensibility that insulated me against anxiety, and my thoughts were bright and clean, with no fuzzy edges or frays of emotion, moving across the darkness of my brain like the tracks of slow shooting stars. It seemed I was receding from my body, discarding it and travelling up and up through worlds tucked one inside the other, like those Chinese conceits of ivory spheres concealed within spheres within spheres. And I had then a premonition not of great danger, but of great life, as if life at its pinnacle were of necessity something catastrophic, something wild and unpredictable, something to be marvelled at and yet avoided at all costs, like the onset of a beautiful storm or the coming of a terrible god.

I was too excited to sleep for long. An hour, no more. And when I woke, when I rolled onto my side to look at the river, I noticed the *waidan* standing on the bank, gazing off in the direction from which I had come. After everything I had seen and done, her blowsy form no longer struck me as unusual; she fell into the category of the known, the dependable. If she had materialized earlier, I might have railed at her for deserting me, but now I was relieved to see her, grateful to have someone with whom to share the adventure. I did, however, ask what had happened to her.

'I took a different road,' she said.

I had learned with her that it was useless to pursue clear answers, and so, rather than forcing the issue, I asked how far it was to the city.

'For you, a few hours' walk.'

'And for you?'

'I will meet you there,' she said. 'Keep to the river and you will reach a ford, a place where there are many palms and the river is narrow. Don't attempt to cross anywhere else. And don't wait for me. I will be there when you need me – not before.'

'You have pressing business elsewhere?' I asked.

'It's best that you find your own way. That is how you will learn to defeat Curtis.'

'You seem to suggest that there are dangers both in the jungle and the city,' I said, after mulling this over, 'and yet you're willing to let me face them without your guidance. Are you testing me again? If so, I'd appreciate it if you'd let me in on the plan.'

She floated over to stand between me and the fire; through her gauzy substance, the flames appeared to be writhing like an agitated liquid in suspension. Her mad hair took the light and bound it into coiled springs, and her pupils were rubied. Her tattoos glowed from within like embers and rippled like worms.

'Did you hear?' I asked. 'You seem to be testing me, and I don't understand why you don't help me instead. I assumed that was the idea.'

'If you fail to survive a walk in the jungle,' she said, 'then you would never have survived the city. And if you fail to survive the city, you would never have survived Curtis.'

'Oh, well, yes, I understand now,' I said, anger flaring up in me. 'I certainly wouldn't want to waste your bloody time! I suppose it would be much more economical if I simply died and got it over with, right?'

She remained silent, and I realized the pointlessness of such outbursts. We were allies, but our alliance was a matter of chance and convenience, and had not bridged the gap between us. Whatever seemed reasonable to her seemed ridiculous to me, and vice versa. Nothing short of a miracle was going to change that. I turned my eyes to the river and watched the spin and tumble of the eddies. Something silvery and quick flashed across the surface and was gone, taking with it the last of my anger.

'I saw the wreck,' I said at last. 'What happened there?'
She replied – stiffly, I thought – that she didn't know.
'Do you know why the city was abandoned?' I asked.

'I only know what the Punan Dayak have told me,' she said. 'Some people came from the sky. They stayed for a while and then they left.'

'People?' I said. 'Were they like us?'

'They build cities, they travel in machines,' she said in an impatient tone. 'They cause fear . . . The Punan Dayak never go near the city. Let us call them people.'

A wind seethed in the treetops, a night thing let out a pining cry. Frustrated by the *waidan*'s lack of enthusiasm, I directed the conversation onto more practical ground. 'Tell me about the weapons,' I said.

'You will have to tell me about them,' she said. 'There are destructive forces in the city – powerful forces. You will find a way to release them. I cannot help you; I can only point to the place of battle.'

'Right,' I said, growing angry again. 'I'll just fiddle around, and if I happen to blow myself to Jesus, well ta, that's all right, isn't it?'

'I have brought you here, Barnett,' she said, making the name into something vile and small, 'because I believe you are the only one who can stop Curtis. I believe you will discover how to defeat him. I feel all this is true, although the longer I speak with you, the more I doubt my judgment.'

'This is quite a different story than the one you told me back at the plantation house,' I said. 'There you were spouting all that voodoo about showing me the secrets of this world.'

'It may be that I can help you,' she said. 'If I can, I will.'

'I've had enough of all this . . . this double-talk!' I said. 'I'm going back.'

'Are you so frightened of death, Barnett?'

'I don't have your advantages in that regard,' I said. 'My fate is still a matter of some importance to me.'

'Yes, but if you die here, then you will be as I am. The *seribu aso* will sustain you in a new kind of life. And you will remain alive for a long time. A very long time. There are worse fates than that, are there not?'

That put a new and startling spin on things, and I asked how she could be sure of this.

'Now that I am like I am,' she said, 'I know many things I did not know before.'

She drifted back into the fire, hanging just above it, her ragged skirt veiled by flame; the ruddy light filled her figure as if she were the glass top of a hurricane lantern.

'Then you must know who will win in the city,' I said.

'Either you or Curtis will die. The rest is unclear.'

'It strikes me,' I said, 'that whoever dies may end up being the real winner.'

'Curtis will not feel that way. And in your heart you don't believe what I have told you. Both of you will fight to win.'

'Maybe, and maybe not,' I said, annoyed by her assurance.

'You'll fight, Barnett,' she said. 'You'll fight for reasons that you may not have recognized. You're a good man for an Englishman. You've been away from your home for so long, you've forgotten how to be an Englishman. You've learned to see and feel in a different way. You'll never be a man of Kalimantan, but neither are you English any longer. It's as if you're from a place that is no place. But it's better to be from no place than from England.'

'You've never been west of Banjormasim,' I said. 'You have no idea what England's like.'

'I have seen Englishmen.'

'Why do you despise the English?' I asked. 'Why not the Americans or the Dutch?'

'To me they are the same. They cannot see or feel. They only do. They're like ants building a bridge of sand and expecting it to last forever.'

I had said similar things myself both in regard to my own countrymen and the citizens of other empires, and

I was perplexed that what she had said depressed me. I picked up a largish pebble from the sand. It was unlike any pebble I had ever seen. Reddish-brown, scored with fine grooves and bearing a vein of brilliant blue crystal in which tiny gold stipplings were visible. Its uniqueness depressed me further, making me feel common by comparison and putting my reactions to this unique voyage into a sickly perspective. So far, I had experienced a variety of personal satisfactions and little else. Here, where even pebbles were objects of wonder, I had mostly marvelled at my capacity for enjoyment, and had given no study to what I was trying to do, except in terms of my survival. For me the place had the potentials of a theme park, a wilderness resort. And if I survived, I thought, perhaps I should rape the bloody place, set up souvenir stalls and sell trifles, ice cream sandwiches, models of the wrecked ship. Run tours of the alien city. Why not? Doubtless I would derive immense pleasure from the process. I heaved the pebble into the river; it sent up a glittering spray.

'You may be right,' I said.

'It doesn't matter,' said the *waidan*. 'This is talk, Barnett. It has no meaning.'

'Well, what does have meaning for you?' I asked, annoyed. 'Nothing I suggest seems to qualify.'

'Before I joined you tonight,' she said, 'whatever I felt and saw and thought, that had meaning.'

'Company diminishes you, eh?'

'Talk does,' she said. 'Unless it defines something.'

'Fine,' I said. 'Do me a favour, then. Define yourself. Tell me who in the hell you are.'

The *waidan* spun slowly away from the fire, making a complete turn as she came to a stop beside the riverbank, becoming a glistening sketch against the black backdrop of the jungle.

'Why do you want to know about me?' she asked. 'More curiosity?'

'I won't deny it,' I told her. 'But there's another reason. You and I are engaged in a dangerous enterprise. It makes sense to know something about one's partner so one can understand the limits of the partnership.'

'Very well,' she said after a moment; she drifted back towards me, her angle of approach inclined slightly downwards, so that her bare feet and the hem of her skirt vanished beneath the surface of the shingle. 'My father was the hunter Sidme, and my mother, Tasang, sold vegetables in the market at Lenawesin. I was their only daughter, and when my two brothers both died of fever before their second birthdays, this was taken for a sign that I would be a *waidan*. Knowing this, I was always empty, until my twelfth birthday when I was tattooed and given *seribu aso*. I have healed over two thousand men and women, and failed to heal less than three hundred. I took a lover when I was sixteen, but, because I was a healer, this went against the rule and he died. I have not taken a lover since. Twice now I have travelled to Banjormasim. Once an English doctor flew me to Djakarta so his colleagues could ask me questions about herbs. I told them no secrets; I only wanted to see Djakarta. I prefer Banjormasim to Djakarta, and I prefer Lenawesin to Banjormasim. I have won nine battles against magicians and lost but one. I have outlived all whom I loved. I was prepared to die, and now that I am not to die, I am troubled by what this may signify. Perhaps tomorrow I will understand more.'

She fell silent, and though disappointed by the brevity of this flat declaration, I realized that it had in effect erected a picket fence around an area of darkness and at least made the shape it enclosed discernible, if not lighting it much. I perceived its symmetry, its strong simplicity, and I doubted that I would be able to manage as concise and effective a self-description. Swindler; thief; moralist; liar; occasional lover; man of many enemies and few friends, none of whom hated or loved me sufficiently to kill or be kind; adventurer; grey eminence; expert on expatriate affairs; collector of passports and information, and seller of same; accumulator of small bright things.

The shape of my life was not easily accessible to description. It was chaotic and turbulent, rather like the wreck of the alien ship, albeit far less imposing: an old hard object abandoned on a foreign shore, gnawed at by things that had once been virtues and had now become eccentric monstrosities. There was a wealth of self-pity in that assessment, but I felt it was of passable accuracy. My fascination with the wreck, I thought, might well have been informed by this recognition.

I looked up to the stars, losing myself in the brightness there. And I had the notion that the sky was a black mirror and those billion points of light were a flawed reflection of some still brighter beauty below, an image as fragmentary and inconstant as the *waidan*'s ghostly being, one whose source was a pure form like a planet seen from space, free of boundary lines and ruin and pollution. It seemed I could feel the radiant specifics of the creation that was mirrored up above, that it came flowing down the track of my gaze and into my eyes; and for a moment it was as if I were a wind curving around the world, knowing by touch its heights, its deep places, its continental sweeps of prairie and breadths of ocean, knowing it all with the same certainty that I might were I holding it in the palm of my hand.

'It is beautiful, is it not?' said the *waidan* from behind me.

I was suddenly very tired and let out a laugh that was more an expression of exhaustion than mirth. 'At least we agree on one thing.'

'Tomorrow,' she said after a brief silence, 'if things do not go well in the city, you may find that we agree on a great deal more.'

It rained for an hour the next morning, a steady downpour, yet scarcely torrential, and as I walked, the rain was replaced by a complex of weathers, shafts of sunlight slanting down through frothy grey clouds to my right, a squall line behind me, clear sky ahead. Despite what the *waidan* had said, I encountered no difficulties, and by the time the sun had climbed halfway through its morning arc, I came to a place where the jungle gave out into a hilly terrain covered with squat bushes and palm hammocks; from atop one of the hills I had my first sight of the alien city.

The word 'city' had conjured visions of towering steel structures, obelisks, featureless cubes, a Manhattan of obscure forms, and because of my vivid expectations, the reality of the place was something of a let-down. It was more the size of Banjormasim than New York, capable of supporting a population of, say, thirty thousand souls, and having an air of dilapidation that was also consistent with that of my home in Kalimantan. The tallest structure by far was a pyramid of dark, weathered stone approximately one hundred and twenty feet high that stood at the centre of the colony; the carved heads of feathered serpents guarded a flight of steps that led to a temple-like building atop it. While not so impressive as I had pictured, the city posed a significant puzzle nonetheless; and since there was no sign of the *maidan*, rather than fording the river immediately I sat myself down on a sandy patch among the tall palms that leaned out from a bluff overlooking the river and gave the place proper consideration.

Rolling green hills rose gently away from the river, forming a horseshoe-shaped area in their midst, and the buildings sprawled across both that flat space and the lower slopes of the hills. I could not clearly make out the buildings occupying the slopes, but they appeared to be hovels similar to those that are found in any Third World environment. The buildings on the river's edge – indeed, all the buildings on flat ground with the exception of the pyramid – were fabricated of a dull bluish metal, each worked with intricate designs, no two alike in shape or size, ranging from a sphere not much bigger than an outhouse to a palatial rectangular structure with a vented conical roof that resembled a futuristic speaker grille. Fancifully configured roofs had apparently been the fashion. Rising from the rooftops were forests of whorled horns, complex mobiles, turrets, spidery constructions, statuary – thousands upon thousands of expressions of individuality. Instead of doorways, the houses had round holes set about seven or eight feet off the ground; the holes were shielded by what appeared to be curtains of white light. Most of the buildings bore evidence of violent usage, their walls dented or ripped or, in some cases, utterly destroyed, affording me a view of the interiors; but the shadows within were too deep for me to see more than faint outlines. A few weeds and bushes sprouted from the sandy streets, which were laid out in concentric arcs, but there was no evidence that any of this growth had been intended for decorative purposes; it seemed rather that the occupants had cleared the land in a way that had prevented all but the hardiest of plant life from taking root again.

Like the wrecked ship, the dead city was rife with activity that signalled the presence of faulty, long-abandoned machinery. Beams of light sprayed from various of the houses, showing pale under the sun, their colours indistinct, and twice I saw something – perhaps two different somethings – moving along the streets at a pace so rapid that it was visible as a fiery blur. Above one of the buildings hovered a cloud of dark vapour that, though a fair breeze was blowing, never once changed shape or shifted its position. There were other incidences of activity, other lights, furtive movements that might have been machines in operation, but in sum the activity was less frenzied and more sporadic than that attending the ship, and put me in mind of the buzzing of a few remaining flies about a picked-clean carcass.

It was the pyramid, incongruously antique and ominous among all that flickering light and polished metal, that came to command my attention; and though the *waidan* had not mentioned it, as I gazed at the structure I began to feel that it and not the faulty machines might hold the key to defeating MacKinnon. I had no reason to think this other than the growing sense I had of the alien city, the feeling that despite the high-tech debris and bizarre

92

detail it was a cousin of Banjormasim, the seedy, blighted backwater of an empire that had spanned the stars and, if the pyramid were evidence, also the dimensions. A port where cultures had mingled and in whose sandy streets had flocked the analogues of whores, pickpockets, merchants and exploiters. The pyramid – with its ornate roof comb, reminiscent more of Mayan than Indonesian architecture – was the clearest yet not the only sign of syncretism; those curious roof gardens seemed at odds with the utilitarian design of the metal houses, as did the intricate designs etched into the metal, reminding me of the reliefs on the walls of Balinese houses. And of course there was the most telling sign of all, the classic stamp of oppression: those hovels on the hillsides. The longer I gazed out at the city, the more certain I became of its nature, and the more certain, too, I became that the pyramid's centrality was not haphazard, that it was indeed seminal to all that had happened there.

Perhaps, I told myself, the *waidan* had been accurate in her assumption that I was the man for this job; perhaps I had a natural bent for it. Yet I was beginning to realize that I could not believe a word she had said, that I could count on her for nothing. She had manoeuvred me by a series of diminishing promises until I was in a position from which I could not retreat, and while she had sworn to meet me at the city, I doubted now that she would appear. She had succeeded in putting me in opposition to MacKinnon, and she would leave me to deal with him as best I could. I had been a fool to believe that she, a primitive, could have discerned anything helpful about the technology of the city: its machines would be equally as impenetrable to her as the colours of my thoughts. That this was likely the case did not harrow me as it might have earlier. There was no point in giving in to fear. I had my back against the wall, and my best hope was to proceed into the city and see what I could find to use against MacKinnon. And, too, it seemed I was committed to the enterprise in a way that would not admit either to panic or any attempt to weasel

93

out of the commitment. The thing was there to do, and I had no choice, moral or otherwise, except to do it.

With a sigh of resignation I came to my feet and started across the river, keeping my eyes on the water, which swirled about my knees, my thighs. I did not look up until I was standing on the sandy shore. There was a stinging scent like that provoked by an electrical discharge, and I sensed vibrations all around me, an oscillating pattern of resistances in the air. Directly ahead of me was a house whose wall had been breached. I approached it and, after a moment's hesitation, put a hand on the wall. Tremors coursed through the blued metal, and I snatched my hand away. I touched the wall again a moment later, this time leaving my hand there. A triumph of the will. The tremor stopped after a few seconds as if it had satisfied itself that I was no threat. The designs on the wall were etched into the metal. The detail was so precise and delicate, it might have been the work of intelligent spiders, and the subject matter was similar to that found in the carvings in Dayak longhouses: fruits, plants, animals. I recognized several species of fish, tigers, orang-utans, but there were many creatures that I failed to recognize, some most unusual in appearance, and I wondered if any of these were representations of the builders of the city. The design was framed by the coils of a serpent with a feathery comb adorning its flat head, and I noticed that this motif was repeated on the adjoining houses as well as on the pyramid.

It took me some time to screw up my courage and enter the house through its breached wall. I stood with one leg in and one out for several minutes, painting the shadowed walls with strokes of my torch, bringing to light a number of objects, none of which made much sense to me. There was quite a bit of broken ceramic and crystal material. The one object that had a familiar shape was a life-sized and realistic sculpture in metal of a chimpanzee with crystal eyes that flashed alarmingly when my torch shone into them. I patted it on the head – an act of reassurance, like whistling in the dark – and the sculpture sprang into fluid life, twisting from beneath my hand, seizing my arm, pricking the skin, a sensation that was less painful than a shock. Then it went scuttling away. I flung myself out of the house, falling onto my back. I could see the chimpanzee crouching in a corner of the room, its eyes beginning to glow, the glow reddening; it was making a series of sibilant noises that might either have been speech or symptoms of malfunction. My arm was bleeding badly from a circular pattern of tiny holes. I regained my feet and went staggering down the street, intending to put some distance between myself and the chimp, and then repair the damage to my arm. But I had not gone fifty feet when one of those fiery blurs that I had spotted from the bluff sped towards me and, before I had time to react, struck me in the chest, knocking me flat at the base of a metal wall. I was encased in a shimmering brilliance, and I felt hundreds of intermittent pressures and tinglings all over my body as if some many-fingered thing was probing my legs, my arms, my genitals, even my eyes, attempting to determine my nature by touch. Then, after a handful of seconds, the touches ceased, the brilliance vanished, and I was left lying on the street, staring up at the sun, half-paralyzed with fear.

At last I sat up and inspected my arm. The bleeding had stopped, and all the exposed areas of my skin were lightly dusted with a sparkling powder. I heard a fuming noise and realized I was sitting beneath one of the circular openings that were curtained with white fire. Near to hand was a shrub with brittle greyish leaves. I broke off a twig and tossed it at the hole. The twig was absorbed by the white fire, held in suspension; for a moment or two I could make out its shape within the streaming whiteness, and then it disappeared.

This sequence of events dashed all hope that I would be able to use the city against MacKinnon. I had no clue as to what I had met with on the street or in the house, and I was certain that whatever else I encountered would be no more comprehensible. MacKinnon might run afoul of some eccentric machine, but it would be none of my doing, and my best chance of finding something to counter him, I thought, lay in exploring those sections of the city that were the least alien – the pyramid and the hovels. With that in mind, I retreated towards the river and walked along the shoreline, heading for the slopes of the hills that flanked the city, keeping clear of the blue metal houses and the streets.

Once into the hills I felt easier, restored somewhat to hope by the sounds of nature, the heated smell of the vegetation; but my investigation of the hovels proved fruitless. Despite being constructed of a plastic-like grey material, most had been reduced to wreckage, and it was difficult to distinguish their ruins from the surrounding growth. In those that were still relatively intact I discovered signs of human habitation – ceramic bowls, shaped pieces of animal bone, and so forth – but nothing that would be of any help against MacKinnon. In one, however, I stumbled across something that convinced me, if I had not been convinced before, that the city had long ago been the site of great evil. On a carpet of dust and withered vines lay the body of a woman, mummified and clad in ochre rags, encaged by a lozenge of pale white fire, an unreal cocoon in which she had apparently died. By the way her limbs were twisted, her hands hooked into claws, her mouth gaping, I deduced that it had not been a pleasant death. Along with her inside the flickering whiteness were a dozen mummified snakes. She was too large to have been a Dayak: that was all I could tell about her, for the process of mummification had robbed her of individuality and made her into a simple emblem of torment. In another of the hovels I unearthed a knife with a metal haft in the shape of a serpent's head, and in yet another I found two small coffins of the grey plastic material; each contained the bones of an infant, and those as well of several snakes. Everywhere among the wreckage there were relics that testified to the existence of a snake cult – rings, medallions, and graffiti on the grey plastic in a variety of languages, none of which I knew, some with hieroglyphic characters, all accompanied by crude drawings of feathered serpents. I recalled from my reading that there had been a serpent cult among the Aztecs – or was it the Mayans? Or both? A god by the name of Kukulcan who had taken the form of a feathered serpent. It occurred to me that the alien culture might be the source and inspiration of that cult: this would explain the resemblance of the pyramid to Central American ruins. And perhaps, I thought, there were also similarities to Indonesian sites such as Borobudur; perhaps snakes were of significance to the societies that had constructed those memorials. But I was limited to supposition, for I had never been interested in archaeology or anthropology, and at that time I was not much concerned with the whys and wherefores of the ancient past, aware that the hour of my death was drawing near. I continued to scurry through the wreckage of the hovels, digging frantically, frustrated by their miserly yield.

Late that afternoon I gave up the search and sat on the crest of the hill, taking a rest before re-entering the city and exploring the pyramid. Towering above the other buildings, its mossy stones almost black against the blazing sky, the evil aspect of the building had intensified. It seemed to darken the air around it, to have grown larger, as if some foulness within were feeding and growing bloated on the light. It was the embodiment of ritual terror, or blood sacrifice, and, staring down at the city, I tried to think how it fitted into the pattern of the blue metal houses and the hovels. It might, I thought, signal a human quality or preoccupation that had caught the aliens' fancy – like the shadow puppets that Americans of my acquaintance had made into sinister adornments on the walls of their homes. And perhaps it signalled a perversion of the form. Like Malaysian discos and cargo cults. That, I told myself, must be it. Some mingling of animism and alien voodoo that had appealed both to the subject race and their corrupted masters. And they *had* been corrupted. I had only to inspect my own past, my several addictions and obsessions, the rot that had pervaded my spirit over the years in Kalimantan, to understand this. Of course it was possible I was putting too much stock in the crude analogy I had drawn between the city and Banjormasim, but I did not think so. My sense of the place had become acute, and I felt that, in seeing it, I was looking into a strange mirror, one that did not reflect any familiar image, yet instead reflected an essence. This kind of introspection was, I realized, doing me little good, but then I doubted that anything I found inside the pyramid would do me any greater good. What could I expect to find? Fragments of ritual implements, perhaps, or some thousand-year-old bloodstains. Nothing more, surely. Still, my two choices were to explore the ruin or else to throw myself upon MacKinnon's dubious mercies. I saw no merit whatsoever in the latter choice, and so, fuelled by these desolate insights, I set off down the hill.

Unlike the layout of the Mayan archaeological sites that I had seen in photographs, there was no open ground left surrounding the pyramid; it appeared to have been dropped from the sky into the centre of the city without regard for safety, and should it be lifted up, I thought, one might discover a number of squashed metal houses. The absence of ceremonial setting pointed up the syncretism involved: it might have been that the aliens' concept of spatial relations did not incorporate the idea of ceremonial space, or else they might have deemed the pyramid's height a sufficiently ennobling distinction. It was cool in the shadow of the building, and imagining that the blackness of the stones was seeping into the air, that I was breathing it in, I was unable to repress a shudder. The stones were fitted together without mortice and, as I have said, were weathered and furred with moss. They were darkened further by scorch marks along their edges, and this made it apparent that intense heat had been part of the process that had cut them. The feathered serpents guarding the steps that led up to the temple were head-high, with glaring eyes and fanged mouths. The steps themselves had such a sharp angle of ascent that, standing at the bottom, I could not see the roof comb atop the temple; each step was scarcely more than half the length of my foot, and they were worn down in the middle by the tread of God only knew how many thousands of feet. I was not eager to make the climb, and in the hope of locating another means of entry, I started around the side of the pyramid. But as I reached the corner of the building, I suffered what I at first assumed to be an attack of vertigo. The houses around me rippled and faded, but did not fade utterly, attaining a miragelike transparency, and through them I saw MacKinnon standing on the riverbank, about fifty or sixty feet away beside a rocky wall, gazing at the ashes of a campfire. I recognized the spot to be the shingle where I spent the previous night. He glanced up sharply at me, and I knew that he could see me, knew that, just as had happened on the rope bridge outside Tanjung Segar, a combination of drugs and intent had drawn us together. I could not make out his expression, yet for a second I could have sworn that he was going to wave at me. But he remained motionless, held, it seemed, in the grip of some tension. Then an instant later the vision was whisked away, and I was wholly back in the city.

By my reckoning, there was less than an hour's light left, and I did not think that MacKinnon would risk a walk in the dark. That would give me about twelve hours to prepare. Twelve weeks might have been sufficient, but twelve hours . . . I might as well not waste the effort, I told myself. It would be more useful to sit down and make my peace with God or the Devil, or whatever dread majesty it was that I sometimes apprehended lurking just around a dark corner from my soul, waiting to mug me. Or else, I thought, even at this late date I might, with the proper presentation, come up with an argument that would persuade MacKinnon to spare me. I continued walking around the pyramid, but I had become more interested in the potentials of reasonable discourse than those of battle. And so, on spotting a tunnel that entered the base of the pyramid at its rear, I did not become overly excited.

The tunnel was only a bit wider than my shoulders, curving up and to the right. My torch showed that a bend occurred about six or seven feet in. I decided that it could do no harm to poke around a bit, but after reaching the bend and crawling upwards for several feet more, scraping my knees, becoming covered with cobwebs, my hands begrimed with a thick, tarry substance, I rethought my options. It was hot in the tunnel, reeking with the thick, musty scent of dead bats and mice and lizards, and so cramped that I was forced to worm my way along. The air, though dry and dusty, felt sticky in my lungs. I could feel the tons of rock pressing down from above and had the notion that I had invaded a magical heap of stones, that at any moment the tunnel might seal itself shut, encysting me forever. I imagined tremors, vibrations, bassy hums, and I had the urge to cry out. The torch illuminated a new turning every ten feet or thereabouts, and it seemed the tunnel was corkscrewing aimlessly through the pyramid rather than burrowing towards a logical goal. Yet I continued onwards, afraid that the walls were about to close in and fit stony muffles to my mouth and eyes.

The minutes were long sweaty exertions, and after approximately fifteen of them I told myself that it was ridiculous to go on. The problem was, however, many of the turns behind me were angled so sharply, I was not sure I would be able to negotiate them in reverse – not without serious injury. I pictured myself hopelessly wedged with a fractured leg, the torch broken, serpents smelling the blood and oozing towards me through the cracks. Something ran across my hand. I let out a screech, and in recoiling from the touch I nearly knocked myself unconscious with a blow to my head. Actinic dazzles pricked the darkness, and the back of my head felt aglow with pain. I wriggled forwards onto a relatively flat surface to rest for a moment and attend my injury. There was already a lump. This was insane, I thought. The tunnel must have been part of a drainage system, something on that order, and might never have led anywhere. Dangerous or not, I would have to go back the way I had come. The flatness of the spot where I was lying gave me to wonder if I might not be able to move ahead a little way and then turn around: that would afford me better chance at a safe return. After inching a couple of feet forwards, I discovered that indeed this was the case. The space between the walls had widened appreciably, and I was able to lift myself into a crouch. The torchlight showed a section of wall approximately twenty feet away. Puzzled by the extent of the clear space ahead, I moved forwards again. The floor sloped upwards, and soon I found myself standing in a small room. I was so grateful for this unexpected relief, I felt like dancing. Yet a moment later I became anxious once again as I realized that I must be about sixty feet up, dead centre of the pyramid, a tiny black vacuum at the heart, and that the ominous humming I had been hearing was not imaginary.

I switched off my torch and stood listening. The sound did not now seem so much a hum as it did the raspy, articulated breathing of something big, rising and falling in pitch. After listening for a while, I began to think that it was organic in nature, and the thought of the monstrosity that might be producing it made my knees weak. Once again I considered turning back, but only in passing: I was becoming resigned to the fact that I would not survive, and I decided that I might as well face whatever awaited me.

There was an opening in the far wall of the room, not a corridor, but higher and straighter than the channel I had already traversed, and I set out crawling along it. Despite the sonority of the breathing, I felt embedded in a ringing stillness, like that which ensues once the reverberations

101

of a struck gong have faded beyond the range of the
audible. Twenty feet along the tunnel I reached a flat
stone blocking my way. I laid down the torch and put
my shoulder against the stone. It shifted the slightest
bit. I pushed and pushed, succeeding in moving it a
couple of inches, becoming winded in the process. When
I stopped to rest I switched off the torch and noticed an
intense white light streaming through minute cracks left
by the imprecise fit of the stone blocking the tunnel. The
breathing had grown markedly louder, and I considered
it probable that, if I were able to move the stone aside, I
would discover whatever unpleasantness fate had in store.
I rethought the wisdom of my decision, but once again I
concluded that there was little point in putting things off,
and I put my shoulder to the stone again. I braced my
feet against the tunnel wall, heaving with all my strength,
and the stone swung inwards, causing me to spill forward
into the light. I let out a squawk, afraid that this was a
trap, that I would continue to fall into a bottomless pit;
but instead I went sprawling in a wide upward-slanting
corridor of pitted grey stone that admitted to a room some
fifty feet ahead. From my position within the pyramid I
suspected that the room must be connected with the
temple that topped the building. There was, I saw, no
light source. The corridor was simply filled with white
radiance. The breathing was louder than ever, but it,
too, had no apparent source. Despite these unnerving
discoveries, knowing that I was no more than fifty feet
away from the sky did wonders for my confidence, and
I hurried along, eager to feel the wind and see the stars.
However, I had gone only five or six paces when one
of the stones gave way beneath me and I dropped into
emptiness.

In the instant that I fell, I had a glimpse of what lay
below and knew I was a dead man. A gigantic green
serpent lay coiled at the bottom of the bowl-shaped
chamber that had been revealed, its plumed head lifted
some forty feet into the air, showing its yellowed fangs.

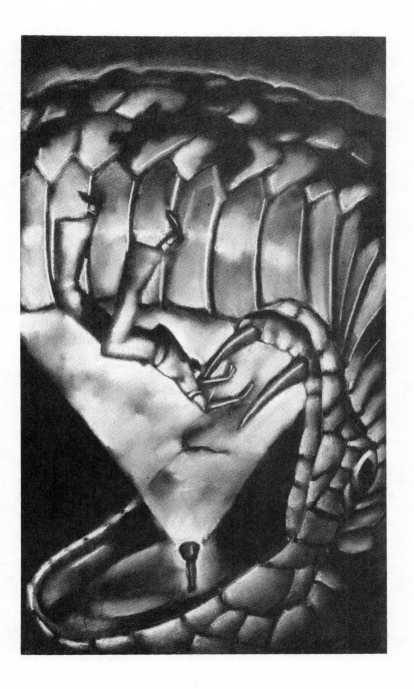

The mouth was large enough to swallow ten of me, the head wider than I was tall. I would have expected, had I been able to articulate my fear, that the impact alone would have killed me, but something, some elastic resistance, broke my fall, and, though I landed heavily, I did not lose consciousness. I squeezed my eyes shut, steeling myself against the pain of being torn apart. Dust covered my face, clotted my mouth, and I could still hear the breathing noise. After a few seconds I cautiously opened my eyes. The sourceless white light filled the chamber, and at first I could not understand what I was seeing. Frays of poisonous green leathery stuff hung down around me, like rips of a decayed garment, and beyond, curious white circles of ivory or stone receded into a dim curving tunnel filled with swirling dust. It was only after managing to clear my head that I understood that I was inside the snake – I had crashed through the dried leather of its skin and was lying within the coiled tube of its dead body, staring at the circuit of its ribs. The patina of dust caked with the sweat on my face was likely a residue of desiccated skin destroyed by my fall. For some reason this realization panicked me as much as had the prospect of a living snake. I jumped up and went floundering away, in the process destroying more of the body, adding another layer of dust to that already adhering to my skin. I beat at the dead husk, the frail bones, grabbing handfuls of dust and screaming, throwing myself this way and that, as disgusted as I might have been had I fallen into a river of maggots. At length I gave up this useless flailing and stood gazing out into the chamber between the brittle circlets of exposed rib. The snake's head was propped against the wall and not, as I had thought, lifted in fury. Its plume was a ruffle of skin erected from the top of the head; its eyes were lidded puckers and its tongue a shrivelled black ribbon forked at the end. The smallest of the scales – some the green of tarnished brass, others a riper shade – was larger than my head, and, judging by the width of the body, I estimated that stretched out it must attain several

104

hundred feet in length. I could not escape the feeling that were I to turn my back, the thing would come to life and rip me apart.

But my real enemy was the chamber itself, not the snake. The stones had eroded sufficiently so as to leave handholds on the walls, and I would have no great difficulty in climbing up; but the stone that had swung down to drop me into the chamber was situated at the mid-point of the ceiling, and I had no way of reaching that gap, unless I were to walk upside-down like a fly. I decided to climb up in any case and learn if any of the other stones could be shifted. In order to cross to the wall, I was forced to walk not across the snake's body, which was too dry and frail to bear my weight, but through it, beating bone and skin into power, cutting a swathe through the coils. By doing so I must have created a structural imbalance, for, as I drew near the wall, the snake's evil head wobbled and came crashing down on me, imploding on impact, eliciting another scream and covering me with more dust and scraps of skin. Dead though I knew it was, the sight of those huge fangs and blind eyes swooping down as if to strike unnerved me completely, and it took me several moments to recover my poise after the dust had settled.

Upon climbing the wall, I found that I was unable to move any of the ceiling stones, but as I glanced in frustration back into the chamber, I spotted a circular opening at floor level – it had previously been obscured by a portion of the snake that had crumbled away. I clambered down, peered along it, and to my great relief saw a patch of stars and black sky at the far end. I retrieved my torch and hurried along the passageway, which slanted upwards at an extreme angle. On emerging, I found that I was approximately thirty feet below the temple set atop the pyramid. I sat on the steps to gather my composure, trying to put into perspective all I had seen, looking out over the city, which was a far more impressive sight by night than by day. The sprays of colour shooting up from the breached rooftops showed as plain as fireworks against the blackness, intermittently bringing to light the intricate carvings on the side of the houses, and those strange quick presences racing through the streets were visible as streaks of brilliance, reminding me of stars portrayed by time-lapse photography. There was something peaceful to the rhythms of those silent pyrotechnics in the midst of the jungle, and, watching them, I began to feel restored, able to contemplate my next move. No matter how loathsome the prospect, I knew I would have to re-enter the pyramid. For one thing, I wanted to learn the nature of the breathing sound, and, for another, I thought if I could block off the passageway through which I had exited, I might be able to lure MacKinnon into the pyramid and trap him in the chamber with the mummified snake. I wished I had a capacity for resignation that would allow me to drink in the beauty of this new world and calmly await the inevitable, instead of spending my last few hours scurrying about like a frightened ant; but I was as yet too much a part of that old grasping, violent, disorganized world to submit to fate.

I studied the the temple, a squat little structure with trapezoidal windows and door, the enormous roof comb rising twice its height above. It seemed the face of the pyramid, hollow-eyed and brooding, a square, stone skull, and – still able to hear the breathing noise, albeit faintly – I imagined I could feel the bitter respiration of long centuries on my skin, a foul wind that bore the anxieties of thousands of victims. It was probable, I thought, that the snake had been fed with the flesh of sacrifices, and it was logical to assume that a good many of those sacrifices had been human. I wondered if it had been the aliens who had brought this passion to the earth and taught it to the bloody-minded tribes, or vice-versa. Such was my opinion of my fellow man that I could not dismiss the latter possibility.

I was still engaged in summoning up the nerve to re-enter the temple when I noticed a luminous speck of white flickering high above the city. Initially I supposed this to be involved with the lights spraying up from the houses, but a moment later it swooped down, becoming visible as the glowing image of a bird or a bat, or perhaps – and this proved to be the case – a cross between the two. I realized I had been wrong in my assumption that MacKinnon would not want to risk a night walk. The thing glided towards me. Its wingspan was enormous, and its ratlike face sported bleak, bulging eyes and horrid fangs. It was insubstantial-looking, like a chalk sketch come to life – anatomically correct, though simplified – yet I could feel the breeze of its wings, and its keening assaulted my ears. I flattened against the steps and began wriggling up towards the temple. Overhead, my attacker had reached the top of its arc and was looping back for another pass. It appeared to be growing more solid, the chalky whiteness of its flesh developing sinewy detail, and I knew that, if it struck with its fangs or seized me in the spidery claws attached to its wings, I would suffer a far greater injury than I had when the white hawk had sliced my palm.

I turned onto my back, thinking I might be able to beat it off, preferring that to letting it slash me from behind; and as it came swooping down again, screaming its thin, terrible scream, the leathery mask of its demon's face intent upon me, the beam of my torch struck it full in the eyes. Light spread like oil over those bulging surfaces, and the thing emitted an even louder scream and went spiralling upwards, blinded and out-of-control. I scrambled up and tottered on the edge of a step, nearly overbalancing.

'Barnett!' MacKinnon shouted from somewhere below.

I scanned the terrain, but was unable to spot him.

'Come down, Barnett!' There was fury in his voice.

I experienced a touch of vertigo as I retreated up the slope of the pyramid towards the temple, still peering down into the darkness of the city. It was odd – I felt less afraid at that moment than I was weary of fear, all my desperate capacities overborne.

'Damn it!' Barnett shouted. 'I want to talk to you!'

The blackness within the temple looked solid and tarry. The torch revealed only bare stone, a few weeds sprouting from the cracks, but there was another, larger room beyond, and from the downward slant of its floor and the faint white glow that manifested when I switched off the torch, I guessed that it must be the room I had seen just before I had fallen. I had an uneasy feeling, yet, hoping that I might find somewhere to hide, I stepped inside, examining the walls and floor in the light of the torch. There was nothing in the first room, no relics, no altar, only the sound of laboured breathing. But in the second room, faintly lit by the glow from the passage beyond, I found a weapon resting in a niche in the wall. It was not a subtle alien weapon such as the *waidan* had led me to expect, but a primitive earthly tool: a dagger with a golden hilt carved to resemble a feathered serpent, likely an instrument of ceremonial dispatch. The blade was about seven inches long and not so rusted as to be unserviceable. I doubted MacKinnon would permit me to come close enough to use it, but nevertheless I was delighted to have stumbled across it.

As I set my hand to the dagger, the breathing noise stopped . . . stopped dead. I glanced from side to side, prepared for the worst. But I saw nothing menacing. MacKinnon's braying voice violated the hush, calling my name again. Without further thought, I plucked the dagger up and was astounded to discover that it had been lying not on stone, but upon a dagger-shaped section of transparent glass or plastic; behind the plastic lay an array of coloured lights whose flashing and intricate configuration were redolent of electronic or digital circuitry. I stuck the dagger into my belt, and at that instant the light began to brighten – not just to brighten, but to accumulate, to pour into a whirling pillar of white fire that formed in the middle of the room and soon reached from floor to ceiling. Within seconds I could make out an indefinite darkness at the heart of the fire, like a flaw in a gemstone. I backed

108

into the front room. The darkness at the centre of the fiery pillar was acquiring a manlike shape – manlike in the sense that it appeared to be standing upright. As the figure solidified, the light grew increasingly bright, rather than, as I would have thought, dimming. I had, you see, concluded that the light was a vehicle for some animal essence which, triggered by my actions, was being restored to its original state, given substance by a molecular spell contained in the light; but although the light was, indeed, involved with the thing's existence, I now think that it was simply a part of its body, something akin to a visible aura, and its materialization was due to another, even more unfathomable process cued by my lifting up of the dagger.

Before long, I was forced to shield my eyes against the glare, and my view of the creature encased in the light became intermittent, fragmentary, because of the rays that sprayed out around it, giving it the look of a lost soul dissolving in the fierce radiations of hell. The figure was moving – of that much I was sure – and there was nothing human about its movements. They were strangely articulated, as if joints were incredibly complex in their alignment. There was something wrong with the head; it was only a shadow in the light, but I could tell it was elongated and far too large to be a man's. And then, for a fraction of a second, no more, I saw the thing clearly.

It was not that the light dimmed appreciably, allowing me clear sight, but rather that the figure appeared to grow suddenly, to stretch and – briefly, partially – to escape its brilliant confine, as if its bones and tendons and flesh had an uncanny malleability. Ghoulishy underlit by the glow that surrounded the body, the head was shaped roughly like a pyramid turned on its side, a pyramidal wedge, and the skin was a mottled greenish-black; it had a wet, new shine that in some spots had the appearance of chitin, yet in places where it fell away from the skeleton it was dimpled and crinkled like old fragile leather. There were two mouths set one above the other – or orifices that I

109

assumed to be mouths. The lower was a lipless slice that vibrated open and closed, giving the impression that it had something to do with respiration, and the upper was a wide gash across which spread a sparkling, glutinous membrane that alternately dissolved and reformed. Drops of shiny stuff fell from the membrane onto the floor and sizzled, making me wonder if – instead of teeth – the creature utilized acids to break down food in its mouth. A number of nubbly, pebbled projections rose from the skull, and when that evil head swung towards me liquid seeped from them, then misted into the air, becoming a barely perceptible haze that spread around it. As far as I could determine, the creature was eyeless, blind, the head having a monstrous, unfinished look, yet I knew it must be able to perceive me in some way – perhaps through the agency of the haze, perhaps the cloud of particles afforded it a means of perception. I cannot be sure. But I sensed the hateful intensity of its regard and felt a flash of cold penetrate my flesh, which I believed to be the shining forth of some chill scanning process and not the result of a fearful reaction. With a liquid, crunching sound, the head began to expand further, to become oblate, the upper mouth widening, and terrified by this impossible sight, I scurried out onto the top step, the beam of my torch veering wildly up into the dark sky. Without concern for my footing, I went tripping down the side of the pyramid, skidding on the slick stones, scraping my hands as I grabbed for purchase at the carved serpents' heads that bordered the steps. My breath came in shrieks, my heart seemed to be darting about inside my chest like a maddened animal. I slipped, falling onto my back and bumping down a dozen steps. The torch flew from my hand. I rolled onto my side, but continued to slide, struggling to slow my fall. As I bounced up I tried to get my feet under me, but instead I succeeded in propelling myself away from the face of the pyramid, soaring outwards in a clumsy dive. I screamed, expecting

110

to drop a hundred feet to my death, having lost all sense of location; but before I had fallen more than six or seven feet, I struck the ground and lay stunned.

Rays of incandescent light were spearing out into the night from the windows and doors of the temple, as if the core of a reactor had been exposed inside. Something dark stood in the doorway, rippling in the glare. My ribs ached, and my back, but I pulled myself up and set out in a weaving run along the rows of metal houses and towards the river. Something heaved up from the darkness ahead. I supposed it to be another of MacKinnon's illusions, but I kept going, not because I was more afraid of the creature atop the pyramid than of anything MacKinnon could summon, but because I felt so frail and rickety, I had the idea that if I were to stop or switch direction, the abrupt shift in momentum would break the threads that were holding me together. I let out a yell as I drew near the shadowy thing, a hoarse cry of defiance, and, forgetting the dagger tucked into my belt, I swung my arm in incompetent aggression, the feeble blow of an old man who felt every minute of his years, and bulled ahead, hoping I would pass through some gauzy, as yet unformed spirit creature and reach the safety of the river. But something caught my arm, swung me up against a metal wall, and I was startled to discover that no illusion had captured me, but MacKinnon himself.

He pushed his bearded face close to mine. His eyes were agleam in the half-light; white showed all around the pupils. His lips were drawn back, and his teeth bared. I could not tell if the expression communicated fear or displeasure.

'What the fuck's going on?' he asked, grabbing a fistful of my shirt. 'What's that light?'

'Something's up there!' I said. 'Some kind of animal.'

I tried to yank free, but he shoved me back.

'What kind of animal?'

'I don't know!'

Once again I tried to break free. MacKinnon slammed

111

me against the wall, banging my head on the metal.

'You don't tell me what's happenin', man,' he said, 'I'll break your fuckin' neck.'

I stammered out the gist of what I had witnessed atop the pyramid, and to my amazement MacKinnon seemed not afraid, but pleasantly surprised and full of wonderment.

'I'll be damned,' he said, glancing up at the pyramid. 'Think it's one of 'em?'

I was confused by his attitude and eager to impress upon him the urgency of the situation. 'I don't know what the hell it is, but we have to get away from here!'

He continued gazing at the pyramid. The thing in the light was beginning to descend the steps. 'I bet it's one of 'em,' he said. 'The fuckers who built this place.'

'For God's sake!' I said. 'Don't you understand? We can't stay here, we've got to – '

'Just shut the fuck up, Barnett,' he said. 'You've been a pain in the ass ever since you got here. I've about had it with you.'

I met his eyes, and what I saw there, anger yet not murderous intent, made me think that he was still withholding judgment, that my execution was not a *fait accompli*.

'C'mon,' he said, pushing me ahead of him towards the river. 'We're gonna give that son of a bitch a run for his money.'

It has been my experience that courage depends on witness, that without someone present whose respect they wish to command, men tend more easily to surrender to fear. I have found this particularly true of Americans. With their tradition of the cowboy mentality, it seems they are able to slip into the role of a strong, silent protector with far greater facility than their European cousins, who utilize more sophisticated models upon which to drape the cloth of their bravado. I am certain that this capacity for role-playing was largely responsible for MacKinnon's initial attitude, and that confidence in his powers was not so much a factor, for he had no idea of the powers accessible to the creature with which he was about to do battle, no idea as well of its vulnerabilities, yet he maintained a pose of calm competence as we retreated from the city, and just once was a crack discernible in his veneer. On that occasion he looked at me and appeared to gain confidence, as if my weakness were a caulking that had shored up his strength.

We forded the river and climbed the rise from which I had surveyed the city the previous morning. From its summit we could see the creature moving through the streets in its cloud of radiance, its dark form evolving and changing as it approached the river; like watching a little boiling drama under a hot spotlight. Wrongly or rightly, I had accorded the creature the singlemindness and lack of autonomy of a watchdog, and I had hoped that the river might present it with a boundary that it could or would not cross. Indeed, this seemed the case at first, for it stopped at the river's edge as if confounded by the water. But it became clear that it was merely preparing for a confrontation. As we lay atop the rise, staring down at the thing, at the shifting black puzzle of its shape within the light, a glowing red cube about the size of a small suitcase materialized in the air beside it and began slowly to revolve. Moments later another cube materialized, this one slightly larger and more towards the violet end of the spectrum. Then another appeared, and another yet, until nine of them were floating in a ragged oval about the creature, all in varying shades of red. Their edges were blurred, shifting with hot colour, making it seem that they were comprised of energy or light. I did not like the look of them; I suspected that they were a weapon of some sort, and MacKinnon must have shared my view, for he tugged at my arm, then drew me into the cover of the scrub that covered the slope of the rise. There he bowed his head, concentrating, summoning his spiritual constructs to battle the creature. Or so I hoped. I also

113

tried to concentrate, to add my focus and strength to his. I had no idea how he was able to manipulate the spirits of Kalimantan – of this other Kalimantan – except that it related to his use of the drug and the resultant affinities; yet I knew that due to my ingestion of the drug I must possess some neophyte ability in this regard, and, bending my mind to the task, I began to feel a myriad vague presences around me, to feel them as one feels the presence of someone who has entered a room and is standing silently at their back. I had an apprehension of their character, not of their individual selves, but rather a general sense of their almost neglible substantiality and of their response towards me, a response I can only describe as longing . . . Or perhaps it would be more accurate to liken it to the autonomic response of a flower that opens toward its life-giving sun. This apprehension of them, however, did not suggest how I might control them, and MacKinnon gave me no opportunity to discover method or means. One moment I was kneeling beside him, deep in study, and the next I was lying crumpled on my side, my head spinning from a blow, with MacKinnon looming above, a silhouette outlined in stars.

'Don't interfere!' he said. 'You're fucking things up!'

As if to prove his point, we were that moment bathed in a lurid red glare: the nine red cubes had popped into being about twenty feet to our left, still maintaining their oval array, still revolving, defining an area of caliginous dark, an emptiness darker than that of the surrounding jungle. I could hear a distinct low frequency hum. A point of light appeared at the centre of the cubes, swelled rapidly, gaining articulation, and within seconds, the point had evolved fully and the alien in its turbulent bath of whiteness stood before us. It looked to have grown, and I could have sworn I glimpsed something bright and wickedly curved at the end of its appendages. Talons, I supposed, in the instant fear took me.

Both MacKinnon and I sprinted for the jungle, crashing through the scrub. Branches tore at my cheeks, my arms, and as I reached the fringe of the jungle I tripped over a root and went sprawling. I glanced behind me and saw at a remove that white node of brilliance on the slope of the rise. The alien was not pursuing us. Nevertheless I set out running again, losing myself in the shadow beneath the canopy, and a half-minute or so later, when I looked back, the light was no longer in evidence. I continued on at a more cautious pace. I could not see MacKinnon anywhere, and though it struck me even then as something of an irony that I should feel deserted by the man with whom I had been prepared to wage war, I was distraught by the notion of being deprived of his protection. I went a few faltering steps farther and stopped, listening for footsteps. Faint stirrings, then a distant cry from somewhere above. These sounds consolidated fear into a cold knot in my belly. I spun about, searching the darkness.

'MacKinnon!' I cried. 'Where are you?'

There was no answer, and I called out with greater desperation. 'For Christ's sake, man! Where are you?'

I thought I heard a whispered response, but at the same moment I also heard a low-frequency hum. Some fifteen or twenty feet away, the nine cubes had reappeared and were slowly revolving. The point of light materialized at their centre. I backed away and fetched up against a tree trunk as the alien appeared. There could be no doubt now that it had grown, outstripping the confines of its white glare, which cast shadows from the boulders and ferns and other secondary growth around us. It stood almost twice as tall as a man, that obscene double-mouthed head weaving and snooting the air like a monstrous hound, drooling its acid saliva, giving by its size and strangeness an impression of evil majesty. The sound of its breath was a loud as a suction pump, and I caught a whiff of an acrid scent like that of something burning. Through the moil of white radiance I watched a section of the mottled greenish-black skin on its side split, making a ripping noise and leaking a clear viscous fluid that added to the slick coating which already filmed the entire body; from that split emerged a

115

serpentine projection, one that soon thickened, lumping up with muscle, acquiring a crude leglike shape. Its steady, twisting extrusion mesmerized me. The way it glistened in its own baleful light. Its rubbery muscularity. Another section of the skin on the opposite side split open, and a second appendage emerged. Within seconds, both had developed into stumpy forelegs, and then, with the ponderous clumsiness of a python uncoiling from a branch, the thing lowered onto all fours, bringing its malevolent head face to face with me, visible now and again through light that boiled like steam. Like the progeny of Cerberus mated with a dragon. Its mouth gaped and drooled, its engine breath quickened. My heart pounded with such force, it felt as if the trunk against which I was leaning possessed a heartbeat. The creature was so much more vital than I, its malefic power so manifest, with part of my mind I believe I bestowed upon it the right to kill me. Then I spotted something shifting behind the creature. A shadowy human figure creeping through the ferns, picking up its pace, scurrying off into the dark.

Seeing MacKinnon reawakened my instinct for survival and I flung myself away from the alien. I ran without thought for direction or pitfall, and I tripped several times, smacked into boulders, into trees. At last I went rolling down to the bottom of a steep, ferny defile, where I lay breathless and full of terror. My hipbone throbbed from having slammed into a boulder, the dagger in my belt pricked my thigh, but I was too worn out to care about these minor discomforts. Once again I listened for movement, and this time I heard a voice whispering, 'Barnett?'

'MacKinnon!' I shouted, afire with renewed hope. 'Help me!'

'Wait a second,' he said. 'I'm working at it. Just a second.'

'I don't think I can walk,' I said. 'I need help.'

There was only the silence of the jungle.

'MacKinnon, please!' I cried. 'Don't leave me!'

A red glow winked on above me, its light suffusing the hollow where I lay, bloodying the ferns, and I heard a low hum. Without looking to see the array of cubes, suddenly energized by panic, unmindful of my aches, I pulled myself up and fled again.

Twice more I enacted this exact same scenario – running myself into exhaustion, hearing MacKinnon's whisper, responding, seeing the red glow and the cubes, running. I was not thinking very clearly, but it had become apparent that the cubes were responding to my voice, to sound above a certain decibel level, and that though they might yet prove to be weapons, their main functions were transport and tracking. I had difficulty accepting that objects of such sophistication would not be able to fix on more subtle emissions, that they would not, for instance, respond to body heat or another form of radiation . . . or, if their capacities were based solely upon aural phenomena, that they were unable to detect whispers, breathing, and sounds fainter yet. And I wondered, too, if this limitation might be due to the creature with whom the cubes were linked – despite its apparent control of technology, I still believed it to be a watchdog, not a master, a brutish thing left to guard the city, and it seemed possible that it was being guided by the technology, that some inherent incapacity of the flesh may have caused the cubes to work less effectively than they might have otherwise. Perhaps a defect had developed over the long centuries. Perhaps the licence governing the linkage of the cubes and the creature was funded by circumstances and principles beyond my comprehension, and there was no real point to these speculations. Or, as I came to suspect, perhaps it was merely playing with us . . . But as I was saying, twice more I enacted this same scenario, and then ran a third time until I collapsed on a flat stretch of ground, at the end of my stamina. The canopy must have been particularly dense, for I could see no stars, only blackness pricked by the swarms of lights that danced before my eyes, emblems of fatigue and adrenaline. I suppressed the

117

urge to cry out, understanding now what would result, and I lay with my senses straining, trying to detect some sign of MacKinnon's presence.

I had been afraid for so long, one might assume I would have become acclimated to it; but now, unable to call out, to vent my emotions, fear became a kind of black compression, a tight muffle sealing me in. I felt I was choking, and my senses grew even more acute. Ticks and rustles and slithers had the piercing intensity of shrieks. I had the feeling that some inimical force was gathering about me, hemming me in, and I drew the dagger I had taken from the temple and held it before me. Finding an unexpected reserve of strength, I struggled up to my knees and twitched my head from side to side, hearkening to every noise, desperate to see what was lurking beyond the limits of vision. It seemed the whole dark night was seething with terrors, yet I could not make out even the shadow of a leaf. I was becoming convinced that the alien had, indeed, been playing with me and now, weary of games, was preparing to finish me off. I let out an inadvertent whimper. A crunching to my immediate left so unmanned me that a jet of hot urine streamed down my thigh. Picturing that hideous thing, its acids dissolving my flesh, exposing bloody scapes of bone through thready matrices of sinew and tendon string, I began to whisper syllables of entreaty, a susurrus of prayer, alternating between exhorting MacKinnon and the creator, saying, 'Curtis, damn you, help me . . . Oh, God, please, deliver thy beloved servant, send down thy light . . .', mixing bits of litany with bursts of Biblical gibberish, making them into a mantra of sorts, staring wide-eyed into the dark and chanting out my fear, my voice growing louder whenever I heard a threatening sound. I imagined claws clittering in the underbrush. A scream was building inside me, like a bubble of black gas trapped beneath the soil of my self-control. Life had become a matter of horrifying degree, and, inspired by a mad fatalism, my prayerful babble came to incorporate curses and taunts. 'Right, you filthy bastard!' I said to the air. 'Right! Let's have done with it, you ugly fucking git!' Then: 'Christ, forgive me! I swear I'll . . .' I broke off, unable to think of a proper promise, a suitable trade-off for salvation. Sobbing, I stood and slashed the air with the knife. I paused, listening. Then, goaded into fury by the ticking silence, I shouted, 'Come on, goddamn you! Come on!' And this provoked a reaction.

First the revolving red cubes, then the alien materializing . . . but closer to me than before, so close that when it shook his head, droplets of acid flew from its mottled jaws and onto my left hand. There was a searing pain in my fingers. I shrieked and flung myself away, falling onto my back. The skin on my fingertips had bubbled, blistered, and the monstrous alien, taking a ponderous step forwards, loomed above me in its inferno of light, roaring, a noise that annihilated thought. The pain was shattering. I screamed and screamed, rolling away into a fern bank, expecting to be dismembered, but there was only a sudden intensification of the light. It grew so bright that I could see its whiteness through my closed lids. When death failed to take me, I sat up cradling my injured hand, still trembling with pain, and looked about.

There was a new source of light in the jungle, or rather a thousand new sources, and the alien, too, was looking in all directions, making what struck me as grumbling inquiries, its blind head questing, turning from side to side, as if trying to determine the nature of the light – something about which I had no doubt. I was reminded of the first time I had witnessed MacKinnon using his drug, how the interstices in the vegetation had been inked in with a black fluid, creating a false night in the clearing where we had been sitting. Roughly the same thing had occured now, but instead of blackness, light had filled in the avenues between the trunks, the gaps between the leaves. Not plain light, but light in the shape of demons, tigers, birds, warriors, and other

119

things to which I could not put a name. Light in the guise of the thousandfold manifestation of the spirits of Kalimantan, forming a barrier, enclosing us within an immense dome of infinitely curious feature. Like those medieval tapestries of enchanted forests whose every shadowy niche and cranny is figured with the faces of half-hidden gnomes and nymphs and trolls, crafty beasts impossible to detect without close examination . . . except in this instance, all the secret figures were illuminated. A vast mural of light and form, given structure by the dark columns of the tree trunks, the forking of branches and sprays of leaves. It was marvellous to see, and not only in that it signalled MacKinnon's intervention.

I was stunned by these apparitions, but not so much so that I failed to take advantage of the alien's befuddlement. Reclaiming the dagger, which had fallen to the ground, and taking care not to damage my hand further, I went crawling off toward the perimeter of the encaging light, preferring the dangers there to those at my back. Twice I fell onto my side, overborne by pain, but each time I righted myself and went on. And as I drew near the perimeter, to my astonishment a gap appeared in the light, melting away faces and wings and claws, permitting me to wriggle through. Once beyond it, I turned and flopped onto my back just in time to see the barrier of light collapse, all its ghostly elements taking wing, charging, or leaping towards the alien and the nine cubes, obscuring them in flurries of brilliant aggression.

There was too much light – detonations and beams and roiling masses of it – and too much confluence of form, of animal and avian and human shapes appearing to merge as they pressed close, trying to rend their enemy, for me to discern much in the way of distinct movement. And besides, I was concerned with escape, with putting a safe distance between myself and the alien. But I glanced back whenever I paused to rest, and though mostly I perceived only a storm of pale imagery, on occasion I was able to catch a glimpse of pertinent action. It was the cubes upon which MacKinnon's spirit army at first focused their attention, tearing at them with tooth and fang, launching phantom spears and arrows . . . Phantom, I say, but still capable of doing consequential damage. Whenever contact was made, there would be a spine-chilling screech, like that of tortured metal, and eruptions of crimson energy would crackle across the surface of the cube; beams of paler light would then shoot forth, and these took their toll among the attackers. On touching one of the spirits, the beam would hold steady and erode the target, be it warrior or serpent or whatever, eating it away until nothing remained. But this process was too slow to be other than marginally effective, and one by one the cubes were drained of energy, at which juncture they dwindled to a scarlet point and vanished. As I crawled I saw two of the cubes end this way, but was uncertain as to how many remained.

I had covered about seventy-five feet when I spotted MacKinnon sitting cross-legged by a mahogany tree, his head bowed, like a monk at his meditations. In the flickering fury of light from the battle, his features looked haggard, strained. I was bitterly angry at his desertion; however, I was grateful that he had cleared an escape route for me, and I derived a sense of security from his presence. Careful not to disturb his concentration, I took a seat a couple of feet away and held a vigil beside him.

My pain had become manageable, and thus I was more capable of witness than I had previously been. Seen from a distance, though no less a confusion of radiance and form, the battle seemed beautiful in its chaos, a surreal incidence of slashing talons and thrusting knives and beating wings, of spirits merging in a grotesque wedding of scale and feather and limb, creating a domelike vortex of vague pearly light, milky white suffused with warmer tints, that muffled the furnace glow of the creature about which they whirled. All this lorded over by the sinister and stately eminence of the trees, like still black gods themselves, with forked arms and leafy minds. The

121

metallic screeching of the cubes had ceased, and the only sound was the roaring of the alien hidden beneath masses of light. I could see nothing of it, nor was I even interested in what was happening. It was not that weariness had worn away the last residue of my hope; on the contrary, I had gained a renewed interest in survival. It was simply that I believed we – or rather, MacKinnon – had won, that the battle, though yet ongoing, was in essence over. I could feel this in the thrilling vibrations that came to my drugged senses, in the joyful violence of the spirits that pervaded the darkness, and I could hear it in the increasingly agonized cries of the monster dying at their hands. That dying went on for a very long time – none of it visible – until at last the spirits withdrew into the foliage, vanishing one by one, all except the shade of an ape, an orang-utan perhaps, though it was much taller than a man and broader than the alien, who was slashed in a hundred places, leaking a sickly yellow fluid. The light surrounding the alien had dimmed, making it easier to see. It lurched to the side, fell, then righted itself, and wobbling on all fours, gave forth with an unsteady rumble that struck me as more complaint than challenge.

For a long moment the two figures remained motionless, effecting a tableau of sublime strangeness and power. The alien, bloodied, its eyeless head snooting up toward its nemesis, seemed compact and solid by contrast, yet also vulnerable and sad – an ugly, broken thing whose course had been run. Towering above it, the ape, its gauzy substance eddying, its blurred outlines wavering, its attenuated arms elongating further, like white rips being eaten in the shadow beneath the canopy. Each of them, beast and spirit, shedding its own light. The dim green crowns of the trees stirred overhead, nodding as if in agreement with an implied verdict. Somewhere a night bird cried, and MacKinnon let out a weary sigh. Then the ape bent down and wrapped its arms about the alien, their two lights, one pale, one bright, blending into a white fire that flamed high to obscure their separate shapes. There was a roar, not of pain – or so I thought – but a final hoarse claim to mastery. This was choked off, and the light faded by half its value. Finally the ape disengaged, and in its pallid glow I caught sight of the alien, twisted and lumpish, lying on its side. Smouldering acids bred thin smokes from the carpet of ferns beneath it, and as they trickled upwards, the ape wavered, grew paler yet and then vanished, as if it too had been smoke, and the darkness of stars and jungle hid the place of battle from my eyes. I felt no sense of relief. I was drained of sensibility, registering only the pain in my hand and my various other aches.

The grey morning sky was showing through the leaves before either MacKinnon or I spoke. He had been some time in recovering, and I had not been able to think of anything worth saying, ambivalent in my feelings towards a man who had saved my life, yet who had done so by using me for bait. That was how I interpreted all that had happened. I believed MacKinnon had assumed that the alien was homing in our voices and had let me lead it a merry chase while he marshalled his forces for an attack. And when at last he did speak, what he said supported this idea.

'Sorry, man,' he said. 'I didn't want to put you through that shit, but I couldn't figure any other way of getting the job done.'

I muttered something about it all having worked out for the best, a sentiment I was not sure I believed.

In the half-light MacKinnon's bearded face was pale, but gone was the evidence of strain that I had seen the night before, and as he talked he grew more and more buoyant in spirits, cheerful as a parson at Sunday breakfast, rambling on first about the possibility of treasure and valuable technology in the alien city, then about his vague plans for the future. It was as if nothing we had experienced had made a mark upon him, and I wondered how he could be so blasé and self-absorbed after an adventure like the one we had shared. Though

123

we were sitting elbow to elbow, I felt miles apart from him, and soon my mind turned from the conversation.

I had all but forgotten why I had visited the alien city and why he had followed me. It may be that he had forgotten it as well, for when he brought up the subject, a half-hour or so after we had begun to talk, with the orange sun showing through the tree trunks on our right, turning the jungle into a panoply of black stark shapes and fiery glares and masses of dark green, he did so in a sober, musing tone of voice entirely at odds with his previous buoyancy.

'Damn it, Barnett,' he said. 'What am I going to do with you?'

A nugget of chill seemed to have lodged beneath my ribs, but I was immune to it, too empty to be afraid.

'Well?' he said. 'What do you think?'

'You want an answer, do you? I thought it was a rhetorical question.'

'I wish it was,' he said. 'But it needs an answer, and I'm not sure I can supply one.' He stared down at the ground, dug a furrow in the black soil with the tip of his index finger. 'I should kill you, but I don't believe I can – unless you betray me again.'

He glanced up at me as if to gauge any reaction that these words might have elicited. I tried to maintain a blank face, and after a second he looked away.

'Shit!' He smacked the ground. 'I don't know what to do. Maybe I should just fucking give it all up.'

My backside had gone to sleep. I shifted, and in doing so, I felt the dagger that I had laid on the grass beside me; it was resting partly beneath my left thigh, shielded from his view. I flinched upon touching it, but then I shifted again so as to hide it from him and ran my thumb along the hilt, exploring the likeness of the feathered serpent, with its golden coils and plume.

'The thing is,' MacKinnon went on, 'I love you, man. That may not make a lot of sense to you. Sometimes it doesn't make any sense to me. I mean love . . . What the fuck is it, y'know? You read about it, you get all kinds of screwed-up ideas, and then you feel something, you try and make it fit those ideas. You think it's gotta be just like what you read, but it never is. So you figure that what you feel can't be the real thing.' He gave a morose chuckle. 'You almost convinced me back at Tenzer's that I didn't love you . . . Y'know, when you were telling me why you helped me. It took me a while to get over that, to understand it didn't matter what *you* thought or felt. What *I* felt was what mattered. And that was the only criteria that counted. You hear what I'm saying?'

I nodded, yet I was not concurring with the things he had said as much as I was with what I wanted to see in him. His face beneath the beard seemed boyish, full of eager sincerity, and I wondered if I had misjudged him by thinking he was no longer an innocent.

'You don't have to give a damn about me,' he said defiantly. 'That's not important. What you feel doesn't validate or invalidate anything I feel. I had to understand that. Once I did, then, instead of exalting what I felt, I had to find what was good in it, what was strong, and I had to learn how to make of use of it. I'm still doin' that, still learning. The more I learn, the more hope I have that I can actually do some good. I know that must sound corny to you, man. And maybe it is corny. But not very many people get the kind of opportunity I've been handed.'

'It's true,' I said, and restrained myself from adding: 'thank God!'

'So what do you want me to do?' he asked. 'Give it up, or try to use what I've been given?'

This, too, I understood, was no real question, though it was not in the least rhetorical. It was essentially a tactic. He wanted me – as he had done once before – to affirm his activism, and if I failed to do so, he would involve me in a debate that would beg the core issue of our conflict, his unfitness, and would switch the emphasis to the question of what choice should be made.

'I can't decide for you,' I told him.

'But you can *help* me decide,' he said, leaning towards me and once again sounding his old theme. 'I need you to help me.'

A wind off the river was moving through the crowns of the trees, making the scattered light tremble over the broken ground, and, possessed by a sense of sad imminence, I wanted to go with it, to be something light and frail and easily dispersed. Listening as MacKinnon continued to talk, to bare his soul, I was coming to realize that he was not reclaiming innocence, he was counterfeiting it – like an actor trying out for a new role, portraying the noble, earnest altruist. Perhaps it was a role that he might someday fully inhabit, and perhaps he did love me in some pitiful, helpless fashion; perhaps my Androclean act of salvage had won some slender portion of his heart. But his love or lack thereof was not of moment in our play. What was of ultimate importance was my comprehension that love in MacKinnon's lexicon was only another form of power, a name given to an area of life he was determined to master just as he had mastered *seribu aso*. He had said that he needed me, and, indeed, he did. Not as an object of love, however, but as a paternal complicitor, as a justification for his assertion of power. It was not really love that was moving him to spare me. His ego demanded that he win me over. And so it was the megalomaniacal demands of his ego that both consigned his moral agenda to the status of an inconsequential footnote and afforded me the opportunity and time to weigh the alternative. Perhaps he had not noticed the dagger, perhaps he had and was not in the least concerned by it. He was so confident, so gorged with victory, he could not conceive of defeat. He was open to me, vulnerable – as the alien had been – to an old villainy whose power he had either not clearly assessed or else had ignored.

I doubt that he knew any of this. Likely he believed everything he told me, inventing new and better moralities as he spoke, charging his least meaningful statement with an evangelical wattage. And sitting there I saw qualities in

126

his face that were not in the least reprehensible. His youth and energy, his delight in his dream of a golden future, the spark of affection he felt for me. All this made my own choice the more difficult. He was, I realized, not a man, but a boy – a boy whose illusions had been perverted, whose basic conceptions had been retooled to permit brutal self-deceptions. Every virtue I apprehended in him was undermined by lustful weakness. He was the perfect colonial. Conscienceless, yet proclaiming the rule of conscience and deferring responsibility for his actions to destiny or religion, or some even less credible spiritual catch-all. And in this he might well have been my son, for I had done the same all of my life. He was no more evil than I. The only salient difference between us was our relative potency.

Thinking this, I felt a sudden outpouring of emotion towards him. I suppose it was love of a sort . . . love or a sense of fraternity or something equally unreliable; and my reaction, after an initial weakening of resolve, was to let my left hand drop down to touch the hilt of the dagger. Of course I was not certain that I would be able to commit murder. I had never killed a man, and though I had assumed that MacKinnon's egomaniacal self-confidence was blinding him to my intent, neither was I certain in this regard. He might, I thought, be testing me. Not that I really cared. If he was testing me, then tests would be the order of the day for the rest of my life, and I might as well fail this one now, I decided, as endure years of fretful expectation. And yet I could find no passion inside myself to fuel the act. Self-defence, it seemed, was not a sufficient motivation. I clasped the hilt tightly; I thought how I would bring it around in a swift arc and drive it into his chest. I adjusted my grip and tensed. But I was unable to act. I lowered my head, keeping a tight grip on the dagger, trying to summon a fury from within.

'All this trouble between us,' MacKinnon was saying, 'all this misunderstanding, maybe in the long run it'll turn out to have been for the best, y'know?'

'Anything's possible,' I said glumly.

'No, really,' he said. 'I mean, I'm not expecting we're always going to agree about things, but, now that we've been through this crap, maybe we'll both understand how fruitless divisiveness is.'

'Divisiveness?' I said. 'Ah! So we were being divisive, were we?'

'C'mon, Barnett!' He gave me a chummy pat on the leg. 'Don't get sarcastic on me. You know what I'm talking about. I'm saying that maybe whenever we disagree about something, instead of trying to thwart each other, we'll know enough to sit down and talk it through. After all, we both want the same thing.'

'And what's that?'

He shot me a perplexed look. 'To save this place, of course. To stop the destruction of the forests. I doubt you'll believe me, and I know Tenzer wouldn't, but that old man's had a hell of an influence on me. I've come to feel. the same as you about this place – about Kalimantan.'

The fiery orange light was giving way to a sweet buttery yellow, birds had started a choral racket in the canopy, and the greens of the leaves were brightening, showing tints of emerald and verdigris and malachite. It would be a lovely day, but I felt none of its serenity, only anger at this mockery that MacKinnon was making of my and Tenzer's old compulsions. I tried to work my anger higher, to build it into a killing rage.

'So in your view I'm to serve as a sort of emeritus figure, right?' I said. 'Your Merlin, so to speak. Whenever Arthur hits a sticky point, he'll come to me and I'll offer sage advice – which he'll accept or disregard according to whim.'

'That's not how it'll be.'

I tightened my grip on the dagger. 'That's exactly how it'll be. You'll come to me, displaying a thespian degree of humility and beg for my counsel. Which, as I approach my dotage, I'll be ever more eager to bestow.

128

God, I'll likely end up so damn senile, I'll actually think I'm teaching you something. And then, armoured by the rituals of obeisance and learning, you'll go off and do what you bloody well please.'

'You're being unfair,' he said. 'You have to give this a chance.'

I paid him no mind. 'Eventually I'll die, and that'll really pump you up,' I said, my voice thick with contempt. 'A tear or two by the graveside. A few drinks and some bouts of soggy reminiscence. Once that's over, you'll be armed with a noble purpose, living up to the ideals and principles of your old teacher. The great wise lump who laid the foundations of your brilliance. You'll blame every fucking atrocity you commit on my legendary savvy.'

Perhaps if he had responded, if he had not maintained a silence, I would have been provoked into striking him. But he only let out another doleful sigh, and my anger seemed to leak out along with that exhalation. In the new morning light I could make out the corpse of the alien lying asprawl in a puddle of sun. Its skin had lost its mottled complexion and appeared to be wholly dark. I could see no detail; it might have been the stump of a tree with spreading roots. The ferns around it were blackened and still smoking. The real monster, I thought, sat beside me. But he was immune to *his* fate, apparently. Protected by the fact that his fate was as noxious a creation as he, and so found itself unable to cast the first stone.

He said nothing for several minutes, and during that time I lost all my murderous momentum. I did not let fall the dagger, but my fingers relaxed and it lay in my hand inert, no more dangerous than a twig. As the minutes passed I began to make accommodations, compromises. Why, I asked myself, should I feel a failure? Killing MacKinnon had not been my idea. I had been cozened into it by the *maidan*, who had proved herself to be duplicitous, the most unreliable of allies. What did I care if MacKinnon ruled the forests or even the whole of Kalimantan? Properly handled – and I knew I could handle him up to a point – this might be a marvellous situation, one that could provide the ultimate security for my old age. All the money and women and power I could wish for. To hell with Tenzer and the *maidan*, to hell with salvation, to hell with every principle except for that of satiety. Why should I sacrifice or strive to the contrary when everything I had ever wanted was within my grasp? It amazed me that I had not recognized this before.

'Maybe you're right,' MacKinnon said at last. 'Maybe I'm not cut out for any of this. Maybe no one is.'

A sardonic reply came to my lips, but the leaden flatness of his voice, as if he had come to a reluctant comprehension, stopped me. He was gazing in the direction of the river, and there seemed a new defeated quality in his attitude, one defined by his blank expression and slumped pose. I could not believe that it was an affectation.

'I've been trying to think,' he said, and gave a humourless laugh. 'It doesn't seem possible . . . to think, I mean. Not without having your thoughts infected by your appetites.'

'And what were you thinking about?' I asked, truly curious now.

'Thinking's probably the wrong word,' he said. 'Remembering's more accurate. Trying to sort out memories, to see if what I believe is true ever existed.' He sat up straighter. 'A couple of years after I left Pertamina, I fell in love with this woman . . . a girl, really. Laura. She was in her mid-twenties but, as far as experience went, she was a girl. You might have known her – or her father. He worked for the Japanese in the hotel business. He was in charge of that new entertainment complex in Surinda. They were just finishing construction, then, and she'd come over to visit for a few months. Beautiful girl. The incredible thing was, she thought I was beautiful, too. And maybe I was – for her. That's what I was thinking just now, I guess. How weird it is what you can do for other people . . . what you can do because of them. How if it was just you, just for yourself, you wouldn't do much of anything. Y'know what I mean?'

I made a non-committal noise.

'I know it's the conventional wisdom to believe you can't change for other people. Once things started going bad between us, I'd tell Laura I'd do anything, and she'd say, Of course, now that you're not getting what you want, you'd say that; maybe you'd even be able to change some things, but once you had what you wanted, you'd have no reason to want to change. There's some truth to that.'

A green bird flew down from the canopy, beating its wings furiously, then planing out into a glide that carried it towards the sun. MacKinnon watched it vanish against the light. Something about the way he stared after it brought a tightness to my chest. Love, I thought, sweet Christ, love, is it? I believed in the existence of love, you understand, but not in its potentials. Throughout my life – intermittently, I admit – I had tried to act out of love, to perform some miracle of being, to exert enough control over my common urges so as to bring forth a clean ray of feeling that would transform the base metal of possibility into something of gold. All that had resulted from these efforts were failures and betrayals, and a thick sour mental residue of spoilage and shame. Yet I still believed love was in me. Black pools of it, reservoirs secreted beneath the granitic plates of my being. Untappable. A wasted and daunting resource.

'But something happened when I was in love with Laura, when things were still good,' MacKinnon went on. 'I did change . . . and for the better. And it wasn't just that I changed morally. I saw things differently. I'm not talking about how everything seemed beautiful and new. It was more than that. I remember telling her once that I thought love itself was a kind of confession, an admission of who you really are to another person. It isn't something you choose to do, it simply happens. Suddenly you're completely visible to that other person. And she's visible to you. You absolve each other of your sins, your

131

flaws, yet you don't overlook them. It's a kind of perfect seeing. Later on it gets fucked up, but it happens, I know it does. And when you can see that way, that pure, perfect way, when you turn your eyes on the world, then for a moment or a day or whatever, you're in love with it, you see all its possibilities and subtleties. You see how it might be changed, how you might make a change. And you have the power to act. Rightful power. Because seeing perfectly, you can only act perfectly.' He looked over at me. 'I guess I was trying to find something along those lines with you. It wasn't very bright of me, I realize that. Or maybe it was. I don't have much faith in my judgments any more.'

It was like hearing myself talk, like going back in time thirty years and more to eavesdrop on the unalloyed romanticism that had imbued all my actions, listening to the voice of a man who has yet to accept life's black lesson, a man who sees death as a woman dressed in silver and violet, and the world's long suffering as a cause for tears and sincere resolutions. I was sick at heart. Frightened of MacKinnon. And afraid for him.

'It happens, Barnett.' He plucked at some moss on the base of the mahogany trunk. 'There are moments when you can see clearly, when you see the right path, when you know what to do. And sometimes you can actually do it. But it's like you told me, it's hard to live up to those moments. Maybe it's impossible.' He glanced at me again and grinned. 'Hey,' he said, 'I must have made some sort of sense. This is the first time I ever remember shutting you up.'

I let my head droop. My eyes filled, my hands shook. Storms of contrary emotions were sweeping away thought. I could not let this go on, I told myself. I was moved by many things, by greed, anger, love, terror. But whatever my motives, the triggering agent was something I had heard in MacKinnon's spiel, the fluency with which he had rendered the most painful materials of his life into a facile justification. That was how I saw it, anyway. In

132

duplicity he was my equal, my rival, my progeny. I felt an awful sense of responsibility regarding MacKinnon. Responsibility and – though it may seem odd – a trace of self-loathing. And something even more odd. Love. Nothing I can say will ever explain to my satisfaction why I acted. I have spent years in trying to sift truth from meaning, and have only succeeded in agitating myself. Perhaps I am simply trying to gild my actions, to portray them in a compassionate light, yet I remain convinced that love was central to that confusion of motive, that with some fraction of my mind I believed I was sparing him worse than I gave.

'You feeling okay?' MacKinnon asked.

'As well as can be expected,' was my muttered response. 'I'm just thinking about our problem.'

'There'll be time enough to figure it all out.' Mac-Kinnon glanced up to the sun. 'We probably haven't got many hours left here. What say we take a look around paradise before we have to go?'

'Yes, I suppose we should,' I said tremulously.

He got to his feet, pushing himself up by one hand, his other hand catching at the mahogany trunk for balance, and as he started to straighten I stabbed him with all my strength in the stomach, venting my inner pain and turmoil in a hoarse shout. Yet at the same time it seemed that I'd had nothing to do with the act, that an electric charge had shot through my arm and caused it to lash out. Blood spurted over my fingers, and letting out a terrible cry, MacKinnon staggered to the side, wrenching the dagger from my grasp. He sank to his knees, gaping at the golden serpent protruding from his gut, the crimson spill diapering his abdomen and groin. Then he fell backwards, twisting in pain.

To some extent I had caught myself by surprise. I had never been sure that I could actually carry out the deed, and for a moment I remained kneeling beside the mahogany tree, horrified, full of a murderer's panic, the sense that God has witnessed the crime, and yet also

133

relieved by what I had done. By the time I reached MacKinnon's side he was near death. His skin was the colour of boiled potatoes, his eyelids fluttering down, eyes rolling up to show slivers of white. The knife must have found an artery – there was so much blood. I had the urge to cradle him in my arms, to offer solace, yet I was ashamed, repelled by the sentiment, by the guilt and regret that now governed me. But MacKinnon gave me no choice but to offer at least a rude consolation. He caught my hand, clutching it as a drowning man might clutch at a root sticking out from a bank, and drew me close. I tried to pull away, but the fierceness of imminent death gave him strength. He grabbed my shirt and brought my face to within inches of his own. In his eyes and his grimaces of pain I could see all the emotions that I had perceived in myself before striking him. Anger, love, fear. All the violences of the spirit. There was nothing of peace or acceptance. Blood came into his mouth, filmed over his beard, and when he tried to speak a froth of red bubbles popped on his lips. After a second he gave up any attempt at speech and satisfied himself with clinging to my hand, my shirtfront, staring madly, as if attempting to beam some last vital secret into my mind. Harrowed by that stare, I pried at his fingers, but was unable to break their grip. I felt I was falling into his eyes, into the depths of the vortex about which his soul was spiralling. I was afraid, I wanted to beg his forgiveness, but could not bring myself to ask it of him, knowing that I did not deserve it. I gave up struggling. It seemed we were teetering on the verge of a great precipice, maintaining a precarious balance, locked into a tension of muscularity and emotion that, if weakened by a degree, would cause us both to topple. I travelled into the darks of his eyes, borne down and down by the fury of his gaze and the shocks of his dying into the grain of life beyond memory; and perhaps I travelled beyond the limits of life itself, for once I realized he was gone, that his eyes were open and there was only absence behind them, I felt I had been yanked back from some strange borderland where the material was translated into the immaterial, where change was the only constant.

Shivering, nauseated by the blood that slicked my hands, I broke MacKinnon's death-grip and sat up. I had no idea what to do. My purpose, it seemed, had been achieved, and now, thronged with emotions, I felt disoriented by the end of things, as useless and imperfect as a thread sticking out from a cuff. Bury him, I thought, I should bury him. I felt the beginnings of grief, that good rich grief that is the right of the truly bereaved ... not of murderers. And I let out a yell, denying my feelings, wanting to be rid of any attachment to this man whom I'd never really known, yet who was so like my younger self. I came to my feet and stepped back from the corpse. Ants crawled over his cheek, over his brow and blood-soaked beard. Signs of vacancy, of ultimate abandonment. There was something, I realized, in his right eye. A glint simulating life. Probably, I thought, a translucent mite swimming in the film of liquid there. The jungle was already inhabiting him, breeding the designs of decay. I told myself once again that I should bury him. Then the glint grew brighter, and another appeared in the left eye. It, too, brightened, and alarmed, I edged away. A vague whiteness began to powder the air around the body, thickening almost imperceptibly. It was then I recalled the *waidan*'s claim that the loser of our battle would be reborn – like she – as something more than a spirit. I did not want to see it, I did not want to face MacKinnon, to gaze into the accusing transparencies of his eyes and hear him revile me. I turned on my heel and went briskly towards the river, not running, trying to preserve a vestige of righteousness, to convince myself that by my lack of panic I was displaying the dignified rigour of a man who has done what he must, who has triumphed over the frailities of his conscience and performed an inglorious yet necessary duty. But I was fleeing nonetheless, and, though I did not witness the spirit rising from the corpse or materializing through whatever process was involved,

MacKinnon went with me, the memory of his voice a dire whisper in my ear, reminding me of failed hopes and the lie of redemption and – most poignantly – of love betrayed.

I must have walked along the riverbank for the better part of two hours, walking aimlessly and without any sense of direction, seething with anger and bitterness that came to be directed at the *waidan*. She was to blame for everything, I decided. Her betrayal had funded and inspired mine. And preferring hatred to further self-recriminations, to remembering how MacKinnon had died, I searched for a means of revenging myself upon her. At first I could think of nothing, but then as my anger abated, soothed by the natural beauty of the land, by distance, I understood that she had placed in my hands the ultimate weapon of *seribu aso*. Of course, I thought, I had no master plan as had MacKinnon; in fact, I had no intention of doing anything with the drug. I did not have a young man's obsession with power. However, I could make her life miserable by holding it up as a threat, and it might eventuate that I would be able to make some use of the drug, that some circumstance might arise that would require my intervention. I cannot say that these thoughts cheered me. I was still full of revulsion. MacKinnon's death had its teeth in me, and I knew it would be a long time, if ever, before I could shake free of it. But the possibility of vengeance, of perhaps effecting some small improvement in the world, this allowed me to mute my harsh self-judgments, and for a while I walked more easily and was able to bask in the peace and sweetness of the place. *My* place. It was mine, I realized, mine and no one else's. And with that realization I began to consider the attendant responsibilities, the multitude of potentials that now lay at my fingertips.

The sun had risen above the treetops by the time the *waidan* finally put in an appearance, and in its bright glare, despite her rags and the withered configuration of her

137

face, she was a thing of beauty, the crystalline planes of her substance alive with refracted light, dancing with light, with dazzle and prism and molten seam. She was floating above the water at a narrow bend in the river, several feet out from the bank, a spot where the jungle walls leaned together to form a lattice overhead, casting a weave of shadow. The green surface showed through her like the intermittent flashing of an emerald; when she drifted towards me, the sere grass on the bank took a gleam from her unshod feet, and whenever the wind touched her, all her lights flurried and flowed as if her internal structures were being realigned by every fitful gust. I tried to ignore her, but she called my name as I went past, and all my resentments came spilling forth.

'I've done your dirty work,' I said. 'And with no help from you, I might add. Now leave me the fuck alone!'

'You did well, Barnett,' she said flatly. 'You have our thanks.'

I registered the word 'our', but attached no significance to it.

'To hell with your thanks,' I told her. 'And to hell with you and your lies.' I stalked towards her, my fists balled. 'Or were you lying? I wonder now if you knew anything at all about what was going to happen, if you weren't just taking a flyer on me. Where's the machine I was supposed to use against MacKinnon?' My voice rose to a shout. 'A fucking knife! I could have killed him with a knife anywhere. This was all bloody guesswork on your part, wasn't it?'

'I knew you would find a weapon in the city. I thought it would be a machine. But' – she went on, talking over me when I tried to interrupt – 'even though you did not use one of the machines, it was necessary for you to enter the city. We realized you would never kill Curtis back at Tenzer's compound. You had to be in desperate straits, in a place where you were beyond the influence of your' – she sniffed in amusement – 'your civilized rules. A place in which

138

your natural brutality would have the opportunity to emerge.'

'Is that so?' I said. 'You don't know know a damn thing about it, you can't understand what it cost me to go through with it!'

'Tell me, then,' she said. 'Why did you kill him? Are you such a fool to believe it was an act of mercy?'

'Shut up!' I yelled.

'It's true, isn't it? You think you were moved to act by some noble principle!' Incredulity flared in her face. 'You killed him because it's your nature, Barnett. Because there in the jungle, alone with MacKinnon, at the end of everything, you saw an opening, a weakness. Because you finally realized that you could do murder, that you were suited for it. And, most of all, because you knew you could get away with it.'

Wounded by this, I was about to respond, to rail at her, to shout denial, when an old man's voice spoke behind me, saying, 'You know she's right, Barnett.'

I wheeled about and saw Tenzer . . . but Tenzer much changed. Tenzer as a creature of blowsy light and crystalline structure, the illuminated sketch of an old man hovering half-in, half-out of a dusty-leaved shrub.

'Don't let the truth oppress you,' he said, drifting forwards. 'It's human nature. We're all in the same boat. No one's claiming superiority. Least of all me.'

'My God, Tenzer!' I said. 'What's happened?'

'I should think it would be obvious,' he said. 'I've taken the drug.' He gave a dry chuckle. 'And I must tell you, death seems to agree with me far more than life.'

There was no doubt that even in this insubstantial form he appeared a great deal more hale than he had when I last saw him; but I wondered how much of his deterioration had been a sham, for it was clear now that he and the *waidan* were complicitors, that they had conspired to manipulate me. I was too astonished, however, to feel anger.

'What in Jesus's name possessed you?' I asked.

'I didn't have long to live,' he said. 'Months, I'd reckon. 'The drug offered a kind of immortality. I had to stop Curtis in order to get my hands on it. I'm afraid we used you, but I had no choice. I hope you'll forgive me.'

'So all your talk about saving the land was persiflage.'

'Oh, not all of it,' Tenzer said. 'If I hadn't been concerned for the land, I would never have come up with the plan. And it was certainly her chief concern.' He gestured at the *maidan*, who was regarding us both with distaste. 'We were fortunate that our separate aims could be achieved by a single course.' He turned a gloomy look on me. 'I wish I could trust you, but I know what you'd do with the drug. You might not act as irresponsibly as Curtis, but you'd wreak your share of havoc nonetheless. As I'm sure I would have done if I'd had my health.'

'I may still wreak a bit of havoc,' I told him, annoyed by his tone of unctuous satisfaction. 'You have no control over me . . . not any more.'

'Absolutely none,' Tenzer said. 'But then you have no more *seribu aso*. You see, I destroyed Curtis's supplies of the drug as soon as I knew what had happened here. And his papers. Of course you can duplicate his experiments . . . that is, if you can convince him to help you. But after what you did, I don't think that's very likely.'

I glanced about, expecting to see MacKinnon hovering nearby.

'Don't worry, he can't harm you,' Tenzer said. 'I'm quite sure he'd delight in harming you, but since he can't, he's gone off to sulk. It's as I said before, he's really no more than a child.' He drifted closer, gleams and glints coursing inside him, a man of living crystal. 'I'm sorry, I truly am. But I was desperate to live.'

The depth of his betrayal was beginning to hit home to me. 'Why did you destroy the drug?' I asked querulously. 'I couldn't have hurt you.'

'You might have,' he said. 'Eventually MacKinnon would have learned that he could destroy the *maidan*.

140

You might have learned it, too. And then you might have found some cause for doing it.'

'I risked my life for you!' I said. 'And this is how I'm to be repaid?'

Tenzer shrugged. 'It's not so trifling a reward to have seen a place like this, a place no one else will ever see. I would have thought someone with your love for adventure would savour it.'

'It's hardly the equivalent of immortality,' I pointed out. 'You've stolen that opportunity from me.'

He shook his head ruefully. 'Consider this, Barnett. You're not at all the sort to be content in studying the wilderness, in merely watching. For me, I admit, this is heaven. An interminable time to walk and wonder at the genius of nature. For you it would be at best a kind of purgatory.'

'Easy for you to make that judgment,' I said bitterly.

'Perhaps, but I believe I'm right.'

'You believe!' I said. 'You had no right to judge me!'

'Be a man, Barnett,' he said. 'There's no remedy for this, there's nothing you can do.'

'Look,' I said, ready to wheedle, to bargain, to plead. 'Isn't there some way I can prove myself?'

The *waidan* cackled, and Tenzer gazed at me sorrowfully.

'I've given this a great deal of study,' he said. 'For a while I thought we could work something out. I know you wouldn't enjoy life at the compound, but if you could put up with living there, well . . . since I intend to go back and forth between this place and the compound, I thought that when you began to fail I might supply you with the formula. Or else, if you preferred to stay in Banjormasim, when you felt yourself slipping you could travel back to the compound and take a chance on finding me there. But in the end I decided I just couldn't trust you. You might be able to counterfeit dying and thus gain control of the drug while you were still vital.'

'What if I did!' I shouted. 'Jesus Christ, man! Do you really think I'd harm you? We've been friends thirty years and more!'

'Friends!' said Tenzer disparagingly. 'Don't make me laugh.'

'What's so ridiculous about that?'

'You've never had a friend, Barnett,' he said. 'All those you call "friend" are simply marks whom you believe you've succeeded in cozening.'

My response was as much outraged as desperate. 'How can you say that? Have you forgotten everything we did? How we helped one another? We were friends, damn it, and no one's going to tell me differently.'

'I believe that "were" is the operative word,' he said.

'You supercilious bastard! Know what I think?' I advanced on him, and, as if obeying a fleshly reflex, he retreated, joining the *maidan* floating out over the water. 'The drug may have taken away the ills of your body, but not those of your mind. You're senile, Paul! You were a doddering old man, and now you're a doddering old ghost!'

'Sticks and stones, Barnett,' he said, and laughed. 'You'll adjust to the situation. Years from now, you'll have erected some sort of rationalization that'll make you believe you won the day and somehow pulled one over on all of us.'

'Paul,' I said, trying to control my anger, 'you may be somewhat accurate in your assessment of my character, but I've never used you as badly as you've used me.'

'That's true,' Tenzer said. 'I never gave you the chance.' He drifted farther from the bank. 'I owed you an explanation, but there's no point in talking further.' With an uncanny fluidity, as if he were himself made of wind, he began to speed away downstream, his figure belling like a blown curtain. 'Goodbye, Barnett! Sooner or later you'll understand I was right! This place is not for you!'

I cursed him as he went, but he did not reply. He grew more and more insubstantial, until at the last he was merely a flicker of light above the green water. Full of rancour, I turned to the *maidan*, who was drifting now at the verge of the bank.

'Well,' I said, 'any final licks you want to get in?'

She stared at me for a moment, then said, 'There's no end to deceit, Barnett.'

'What the hell does that mean?' I asked.

'It's as your friend told you,' she said. 'Sooner or later you will understand.'

I was too disillusioned to pursue the matter. For a few seconds I stood watching her waver and drift, watching the seams of light slanting through her brighten and fade.

'I envy you,' she said. 'I realize you won't understand that, either. But perhaps some day you will. Take heart, Barnett. You've done the best for yourself that could be done.'

'Right!' I said with venomous sarcasm. 'The fucking accolade was within my grasp! I should be delighted at such a near miss.'

She started to drift off into the jungle, and I went a few paces after her, calling out, 'What's to happen now?'

For you?' Her body intersected a sapling trunk, and for an instant her translucent substance was cored with a shaft of pale green bark. 'In a short time you'll return to Kalimantan. Tenzer's men will be waiting to guide you back to the river. He told them you would be coming.'

I did not want her to leave, or perhaps, despite the fear and the bloodshed, I did not want my stay in that other world to end, and she seemed emblematic of the place, of its inevitable loss . . . and of a loss beyond measure.

'Wait with me,' I said. 'It's just a little while, you say. Surely you can wait with me a little while.'

'Why?' she asked. 'We are not friends.'

'I know,' I said, 'but neither are we enemies . . . not any more. Just wait with me a bit.'

'I cannot tell you how to make the drug,' she said, 'if that is what you're after.'

143

'No,' I said, feeling utterly defeated and weary. 'I'd just like a bit of company, that's all.'

She nodded, as if she were trying to accommodate some new weight of information and it was causing her head to wobble. Then she drifted closer, so close that I could make out the intricate structures of her eyes. It unnerved me to see those crystalline lenses flowing and dissolving like films of glowing ice, and I turned away.

'Look at me,' she said.

'What for?' I asked, suddenly suspicious.

'I want to give you a gift.'

Still wary, I refused to do as she asked.

She laughed, a fey, distant laugh, as if she saw our circumstance in a sad and diminishing light. 'I no longer have any reason to trick you, Barnett. Take my gift.'

'Why would you want to give me anything?' I asked.

'Why is it important that you understand me?' she said. 'You know that you cannot. Look at me, Barnett. It's a trivial gift. It will change nothing between us, but it may make it easier for both of us to think back on this day.'

Her eyes were cluttered depths of crystal and fire, like a garbage of priceless debris. Yet as I gazed into them, as I travelled along them, along those curving infinite wells, the bright shapes within began to take on a semblance of order, to align into a jewelled landscape, a mosaic that seemed at first surreal, but then, as the light faded to an ordinary glory, resolved into jungled hills and a green river whose surface was cut by gliding, crested serpents and, set upon a grassy rise above the water, a group of longhouses, with brownskinned people sitting on the porches and others gathered about canoes tied up to the bank. It must be, I realized, a settlement of the dream wanderers, the Punan Dayak. Seconds later I was among them, an invisible witness, delighting in the proven reality of this emblem of my youthful passion, in the sweet commonality of their lives, the women preparing food, the men fashioning arrows and fish hooks, the children at their games. But as I watched

144

them, I realized that they were not thriving. The tattoos on their faces and chests were not so intricate and fine, the women's beadwork was slovenly, and there was a listlessness attaching to the actions of the men, as if their work was of no real importance but merely a pastime, a means of whiling away the hours. It became clear to me that by escaping the old world, by removing themselves from the pollutants of our modern society, they had also removed themselves from its vitality; and I understood that one way or another, whether through syncretism or decay, their culture had been doomed, and that my faith in the existence of Eden, of cultural purity devoid of the dynamism of change, was as feckless and immature as any of MacKinnon's half-baked schemes. I felt resentment towards the *waidan* for having shown me this and so debunking my favourite illusion. But perhaps, I thought, it was an illusion that she had chosen to believe despite the contrary evidence. Or perhaps not. It may be that she knew what I would derive from the experience, that she was trying to distress me further, or else she truly believed that such a disillusionment was a gift, that knowing there was no better world would prove sustaining to me in the years ahead. I was never able to fathom her motives. She remains the one mystery in all this sorry matter, the one incomprehensible magic. I suppose it is a testament both to my lack of faith in mysteries and to my childish romanticism that I have never since sought to explain her and have chosen rather to treasure her memory, to transform it into something I can take out from time to time and handle, that I can rub and conjure with, that brings back the sweet inessentials of other, less mystifying mysteries. A cryptic talisman that belies the crude reality which gave it birth, like a golden dagger or the faceted perfection of a black sapphire.

Barnett shifted in his chair; the straw seat crackled like the flaring of a small fire. He made a florid gesture and appeared to pluck a sapphire – the same one he had

145

magicked away – from thin air. He held it to his eye and chuckled as if pleased by something he had seen at its heart, then slipped the stone into his shirt pocket. The Dayak boy had lit a kerosene lamp; it cast a powdery orange glow throughout the shop, shining off all the glass surfaces. From without came the sounds of men arguing, children at play, radios, intermittent splashes. Whenever the damp wind gusted, the curtains belled inwards and flashlights from passing boats probed the gap between them.

'I believe that's the saddest story I know,' Barnett said. 'There are stories I might tell that are less hopeful. Stories about the poor, for instance. The starving, the gleaners of garbage dumps, the plague-ridden. But there's no story I recall that better details the lapse of hope and the enervation of good impulse, that puts into sharper focus the signals of our civilization's general decline. And there's no story I can think of that shows more plainly what absolute fools men are to think they understand the twists and turns of an alien shore . . . though I imagine that's not altogether clear from what I've told you thusfar.'

He plucked a pack of clove cigarettes from his trouser pocket, lit one, inhaled and burst into a fit of coughing, expelling clouds of smoke. Once his coughing had subsided, he frowned at the cigarette, then flung it onto the floor and made an ineffectual attempt to stamp it out. 'Goddamn things,' he said. 'I'd give my fucking left arm for a pack of Players.'

The Dayak boy came over and picked up the still-burning cigarette, but Barnett appeared not to notice, gazing at the twitching curtain.

'That was the last time I saw the *waidan*,' he said. 'In truth, I never expected to see either her or that part of Kalimantan again. Two years later, however, I fell ill. I recovered completely, but that brush with mortality had made me painfully aware that my years were dwindling, and I decided to visit the compound in hopes of finding Tenzer and convincing him to share the secret of *seribu*

146

aso. But when I arrived at the compound, accompanied by several local Dayaks, all my hopes were dashed. Two years of neglect had let the jungle back in, and the place was in ruins. Vines crawling across the rooftops, shrubs blocking the ladders, gibbons howling and lesser monkeys scampering here and there. You could just see the roofs and sections of the walls through the vegetation. The fence was shattered, and there was a rank stench of decaying foliage and animal faeces. No sign of Tenzer whatsoever.

'We pitched camp within the remnants of the compound wall, and later that evening I strolled out into the jungle. It was a lovely night, with the usual complement of stars and an enormous moon just on the wane that pierced the canopy with shafts of light nearly as distinct as those of the morning sun. In its light the terrain of boulders and ferny hillocks and mahogany trunks acquired a magical air, everything agleam, bathed in a soft silver radiance, like a world under an enchantment. I had been walking for about five minutes when I spotted a glimmer up ahead, a pale hurrying shape. Anyone else might have given it a wide berth, but certain that it was Tenzer, I hustled towards the shape, which continued on through the trees, alternately vanishing and reappearing. It was moving at quite a rapid pace, and I soon lost sight of it. Rather than risk becoming lost myself, I decided to go back to the compound. But when I turned, I discovered that the object I had been pursuing had been standing directly behind me. MacKinnon. Or rather his shade. With only the moon and stars to charge his internal structures, he was a wispier creature than the *waidan* had been, but his features were plain, and there was no mistaking his mood. He stared at me with a stony expression, and despite the inconstancy of his form, his hatred seemed to strike with the intensity of high beams suddenly switched on. He did not speak, merely kept his eyes trained on me, drifting a few feet forwards and then back or to the side, like a man at the mercy of a gentle invisible current. Now and again

147

he would drift through a shaft of moonlight, and when this occurred, it was as if his form had been poured full of sparkling silver wine, and the liquid was flowing off along a system of devious internal cracks and channels.

'All the horror of which I had been trying to divest myself during the past two years now overwhelmed me. Yet I knew I could no longer avoid the confrontation that I had avoided in that other, alien forest, and finally, hesitantly, I asked, "How are you, Curtis?" It was the first time I had ever addressed him by his Christian name, and this spoke to a desire for intimacy born of my need for absolution.

'"How am I?" He gave the words a blithe, sardonic emphasis and let out a wild laugh. Then, affecting a British accent, he said, "Just fine, old chap! Never better. I'm having a ripping good time." There was about him a ragged feverish intensity that smacked of mental erosion.

'"God, Curtis,"' I muttered, "I don't know what to say, I— "

'"Just go away, Barnett!" he said. "You've caused me enough pain."

'"Maybe I was wrong to do what I did, Curtis," I said. "At the time I believed I had to do it." He scoffed at this, but I ignored him. "Now I'm not so sure. But . . ." Everything I had in mind to tell him seemed a rationalization, and I let the unfinished sentence hang, feeling helpless, raw with guilt, like a child caught at some vile act.

'"Can you imagine how it hurt?" he said. "I'm not talking about how it felt to be betrayed or to know you're dying. Just the physical pain alone. I can still feel it. The memory's so sharp, it's more real than I am." He came closer and bawled, "It hurt!"

'"But you didn't die," I said, rushing my words, trying to soothe him, disconcerted by his obvious instability. "Perhaps that doesn't make up for what you've lost, but surely this new life is compensation of a sort. I envy your potentials so much."

'"You envy me?" MacKinnon made a noise of disgust. "How could you possibly envy this?" He waved at himself, and the edge of his hand sliced into the gauzy textures of his chest. "Only a pervert would feel envy for me."

'"Yes, yes," I said, "I understand it's not like being fully alive, but years after I'm dead, there you'll be, able to see and think and know things. I've no doubt you'll feel differently then."

'"What the fuck are you talking about?" he asked.

'Startled by his ignorance, his vehemence, I repeated all that the *waidan* had told me, and when I had done, he gave me what I took for a pitying stare. Then he smiled.

'"I guess that does make you feel pretty good about what happened, doesn't it?" he said sarcastically. "Makes you feel like you've both given and taken away . . . sort of like the Lord, huh? Like Jesus."

'"I'm not sure what you're getting at," I said.

'"Well, come on," he said, beckoning. "I'll show you."

'I hung back, leery of his intent.

'"C'mon, Barnett," he said. "I bet you'd like to see your ol' pal Tenzer again, wouldn't you?"

'"Tenzer? Is he here?" I asked.

'"I expect he's somewhere around," MacKinnon said; he moved off into the shadows. "He never strays far from the compound."

'"Really?" I said, setting out in MacKinnon's wake. "I'd have thought he'd spend most of his time in the other world."

'"You know how it goes," MacKinnon said diffidently. "Sometimes a man just loses interest."

'I tried to engage him in further conversation, but he refused to respond. We wandered aimlessly, it seemed, meandering, doubling back, and I wondered if he was attempting to confuse me, hoping that I would become lost. But after about twenty minutes I spotted another glimmer between two trunks up ahead.

'"Is that him there?" I asked, and Mackinnon replied, "Yeah, more or less."

'I hurried forward, trampling ferns underfoot. The pale form I had seen vanished behind a massive head-high boulder. "Tenzer!" I called. "It's me – Barnett!" Then, rounding the boulder, seeing Tenzer, a far paler, wispier Tenzer than the one who had taunted me on the riverbank, I called to him in a calmer tone, one designed to hide my anxieties and persuade him of my good will.

'He was bending to inspect a patch of moss on the side of the boulder, his back half-turned to me, and did not appear to have heard.

'I called to him again, and still he did not respond. Perhaps, I thought, he was giving me the cold shoulder.

'"Paul," I said. "I've come all the way from Tenggarong to see you."

'He gave a feeble croak of – it seemed – bewilderment, plucked at the moss and then half-said, half-sang out, "What's the name, what's the name?" He straightened. "Damn, damn, damn! I shall have to look it up. Curtis, would you mind going back to the house and bringing me the reference work on lichens." He was not addressing MacKinnon, who was standing beside me, but was speaking to the air. Then he turned towards me, and I realized that his wispiness was not merely a product of the diminished light. Great holes had been worn in his substance, and sections of his form floated separately from the linked majority of the body – a portion of his hand, for instance, vibrating like a silver butterfly, and a sliver of his cheek trembling like an agitated crescent moon. Where the pit of his stomach should have been was only a glittering haze. One eye was empty, a tunnel through his ghostly skull into the darkness of the trees. "Ah!" he said with daffy pleasantness. "What have we here?" He came forwards, an expression of amiable curiosity fitted to his decaying features.

'I assumed that he was about to greet me, but instead of stopping and acknowledging my presence, he passed right through me, causing me a stab of panic and a needling sensation like one sometimes has when a shot

151

of novocaine is wearing off. He drifted away among the mahogany trunks, and I turned to MacKinnon, full of fearful questions.

'He was grinning like a madman. "She lied," he said gleefully. "The bitch lied to us all; she used us all. And most of all she used Tenzer. He was so sure he'd found salvation. I guess that's the way of desperate men: they clutch at any straw. But immortality?" He gave a laugh that sounded more like a kind of human static. "Not hardly, Barnett. A few years of wandering, and then in the space of a few weeks, you wear away like an old sock. And then" – he waved his hand at the sky – "nothing."

'"But you seem absolutely fine," I said. "Maybe it's only Tenzer who's been affected this way."

'"I seem fine, do I?" He looked as if he wanted to spit at me. "Know what I'd planned for you? I'd forgotten it for a minute there – my memory's not what it used to be. But I had such a wonderful plan." Another crackling laugh. "See, I knew you'd come back, I knew you'd have to return to us sooner or later, begging for the drug. And I intended to give it to you. I was going to pretend I'd forgiven you for what had happened. Then I'd give it to you and watch you dissolve. But the problem is, just as I couldn't remember my plan, I can't remember the goddamn formula. All my memories are fading." He favoured me with another manic grin. "That's the first stage."

'I recalled what the *maidan* had said about there being no end to deceit, and despite my desire to argue with MacKinnon, to disprove what he had told me, I knew that I could not.

'"You can't feel good about any of this, man," he said. "No fucking way! You've killed me; you've sentenced me to this goddamn half-life . . . and that's worse than anything. Know what it's like? It's cold, man! It's cold and sad and lonely. It's dying by inches. It's every damn second looking deeper and deeper into the pit that's going to swallow you up. It's a fucking horrorshow, you bastard! If I could do the same to you, I'd do it in a flash. Believe me! But the worst I can do now is to tell you how it is, to make you understand what I'm going through."

'I took a couple of steps backwards, then turned and headed back to the compound.

'"What's wrong, Barnett?" MacKinnon shouted. "Little hard to take, is it? Doesn't suit your self-image?"

'I picked up my pace.

'"You can't hide from me, man!" A giggling laugh. "I'm always going to be with you . . . even when I'm not there. Always!"

'He continued to shout, to harangue and vilify, but I was so directed towards leaving him behind, towards proving him wrong, towards forgetting him, that his words had no effect other than to speed me along.'

Barnett lowered his grey head, picked at a frayed thread on his cuff. 'But it was MacKinnon who proved to be right. I'll never be rid of him, I'll never put that night behind me. Yet I've managed to come to terms with it in a number of ways. I've accepted as truth that by killing MacKinnon I did what needed to be done. He had, after all, murdered the *waidan*, and I had at worst been his executioner. That the *waidan* used me . . . it's of no moment. If anything, it provides me with another edifice behind which I can take moral refuge. However, it was another night at Tenzer's compound, a night some sixteen months later, that truly allowed me to attain a measure of peace.'

The Dayak boy had fallen asleep behind the counter, nodding on his stool, and Barnett called to him, asked him to make coffee. Drunken men were singing somewhere nearby, and a freshet of rain sprang up, pattering on the tin roof.

'I hate these nights before the monsoon,' Barnett said. 'The days are tolerable, but the nights . . . sticky, filthy. They make me yearn for England.' He grunted with amusement. 'Of course I'd be completely at sea in England. What the hell would I do there? Become a monument at a corner table in some pub, probably. "Old

Barnett, he'll spin you a tale about the mysterious East, he will. Just buy him a pint and stand back!"' He shook his head violently like an old bull troubled by flies. 'I'm not quite clear why I went back to the compound a third time. Some faint hope of laying the ghost, I imagine. There was a degree of resignation involved, too. I had concluded that, while I owed MacKinnon nothing, I owed myself some sort of resolution, be it painful or not. And if resolution was possible, I knew that Tenzer's old home was the place to find it.

'The compound was in a far more ruinous condition than when last I had seen it. Bamboo had sprouted, as had a number of saplings, and these were entwined with pitcher plants. The leaves of many of the shrubs were bound with the larval silk of ant colonies; they had the aspect of large cocoons, and it was impossible to stand near them without being bitten. Pythons lay coiled in the broken houses, and swarms of tiger beetles infested the underbrush. Tenzer was gone. Worn away completely, I suspected, or else he had just wandered off. But MacKinnon was still about, though he had suffered a terrible dissolution and become a man of parts. A section of his torso and his head were still joined, but the rest was a patchwork of perceptible elements connected by a particulate haze. It was on my second night there I saw him, and the sight was hard to take. He was hovering at the foot of the rotted ladder that led up to the vine-choked entrance of his old house, and he was staring at the doorway as if wondering how to negotiate the broken rungs. A decayed phantom of silvery light, with vague flickers in his eyes and part of his lips rubbed away and a cheek of pure vibration. I approached with trepidation and called to him. He did not respond, and I assumed that he had reached a state in which the imperatives of my world no longer had any pull upon him. But after a considerable silence he turned to me. His face was awful to see, displaying the effects of what I thought of as a spiritual leprosy, a composite of dark spaces and glowing sketchy lines, given depth and volume

154

by the moonstruck slants within. The fleshy leaves of a shrub pierced him like dark green spearpoints.

"'Barnett," he said in a tone of mild surprise. "It's been a long time, man. Can I order you a Scotch?"

'I said, "No," wondering where exactly he thought we were, and when, for it was apparent that to his mind we were not in Tenzer's compound, but in some civilized watering hole.

"'A wise decision," he said. "Even a casual drink can lead to seduction in the tropics. You told me that one time . . . remember?"

"'Ah, yes," I said. "I believe so."

'He grinned, a ghastly tear spreading in his cheek. "I'm well on my way to being seduced today, I'm afraid. I believe I've had . . . must be seven, no, eight whiskies."

"'Well," I said, "you seem to be holding your own."

"'Yes, indeed," he said; his speech, I noticed, was becoming more that of a drunk, the imagined situation coming to possess him. "That's exactly what I'm doing. Holding my own." He nodded. "I got woman trouble, y'see. Ever have woman trouble, Barnett?"

"'Nothing but," I replied.

'He laughed. "Yeah, right." He looked off through the gapped fence of the compound, doubtless seeing there the rich darkness of a Surinda bar, with blinding light shining through the doorway, bicycles and motor scooters passing in the street. "Laura," he said. "That's her name . . . Laura."

"'American?" I asked, wanting for reasons I could not fathom to keep the conversation going.

"'Yep, 'merican." He glanced down as though into an empty glass. "I love her ass, Barnett. It's fucking awful." He nodded again, as if agreeing with some inner voice. "But it's great, too, man. I mean, even when it sucks like now, it's better'n not being in love. Know what I mean?"

"'The intensity," I said.

"'That's it," he said. "*In*tensity! Can't live with it, can't live without it." He sighed. "Barnett, you're a wise old bastard, y'know. I really fucking respect your ass. I'm serious. Man, even if you fucked me over, I'd have to sit down and think about it. And I'd probably decide I deserved it, y'know. 'Cause I been watching you, man, and you don't do shit 'less you've got a damn good reason."

'I wondered if he was in some oblique way offering me forgiveness. It was tempting to think that he was trapped in an illusory circumstance, yet somehow aware of our true condition. I was unable to depend on such an elusive absolution, however, and I found it impossible to press the issue.

'He spoke further about Laura, both in terms of his thwarted passion and his memories of a golden time, then – after bidding me a drunken farewell – went weaving off into the jungle.

'I was disturbed by this encounter, but to an extent I was heartened as well. That he was reinhabiting his old love affair might, I thought, signal a gentle and merciful regression. To an extent I believe this was so, for over the next few days and nights he appeared to relive various other events – it was rather like the old saw about having one's life pass before one's eyes, only in MacKinnon's case this process was not occurring in the space of a second or two, but over weeks, as if time had for him become elastic and the moment of death had become a continuum in which he could dawdle and explore. That, too, I believed to be an accurate assessment of his situation, for it accorded with what he had told me on our previous encounter about looking deeper and deeper into the pit that was preparing to swallow him. It seemed now that he had accepted the fact, that he had resigned himself and was making the best of a bad lot, and I doubted he would have anything more pertinent to say to me than he already had. He was retreating into his own world, scarcely aware of me, and his dissolution was becoming extreme. I could see no reason to watch the end, and I made plans to break camp on the morning of the sixth day.

'I spent the fifth night following him about the compound; I had to a large degree come to terms with my guilt, and on this final night, I was more honouring him, keeping a vigil, than attempting to heal myself. For all his faults and inadequacies, MacKinnon had been an adventurer, and there were, I thought, not so many of us left that we should let any of our number pass without memorial notice. His face and head were still recognizable, as were the lower portions of his legs, but the remainder of his form had been reduced to a few outlines and a haze of moonlit particles, and I wondered if what he was undergoing was in essence the same thing that we each of us experience at the end of our days, if the death of the soul is always marked by a whirling of silvery atoms.

'He did not speak to me or confront me in any way for the first hour; he had not done so in two days, and, in truth, I was not expecting it. He appeared to be involved with some old friends at Pertamina, talking about girls and sports, and to hear him laughing and carrying on gave me – despite the poignancy of the moment – a good feeling. But as the moon climbed to its zenith, bathing the compound in snowy light so brilliant that it manufactured a sort of bleached day, MacKinnon drifted very close to me, stared with his tunnelled eyes, and said, "Barnett," in a shocked whisper, as if he had just become aware of my presence.

'I was certain that he recognized me, that his calling out of my name was not part of a delusion; for some reason he had fought his way back to the here-and-now, and this realization shattered my complacency. I was at a loss, incapable of answering him.

'"Barnett," he said again, this time giving the name a softer emphasis, as if it were the embodiment of some treasured conception.

'"What is it?" I asked, torn between the desire to help him and the urge to flee, to avoid further emotion.

'He said something that I could not hear, and I realized that he was beginning to break up, like an old wreck on a reef finally submitting to the battering of the tides. His

157

outlines were fading, the particulate haze that composed most of his body attenuating, thinning, its cohering principle abolished. Under ordinary circumstances I would have been terrified to witness this, and, indeed, there was terror in me; yet I was unable to retreat from witness, commanded by the unstrained lineaments of his face, by his fragmentary expression of calm regard. Within seconds, however, his face had been partially erased, and there was nothing to hold me. I turned and walked off several paces and stood waiting for him to fade, feeling oddly untroubled, thoughtful yet not tormented by thought. There was a seething noise – wind, I suppose, though at the time I imagined it to be the hissing passage of his substance. After three or four minutes I turned back. What looked like dust motes were dancing in a shaft of moonlight that slanted down onto one of the shrubs. There was something pagan and strange about the sight, about that pale distinct beam with its crystalline definition touching the agitated tips of the leaves. I perceived it suddenly as a crowd of tiny green heads and waving hands drenched in the ray of creation, receiving some vital essence or news, or else yielding up the same. And then, as ragged blue clouds passed across the moon, this illusion collapsed, and I knew that I was finally alone.'

Barnett started to light another cigarette, but thought better of it and tossed the pack onto the floor. A reedy piping began in the adjoining shanty, an oboe or a snake-charmer's flute, weaving an ululating, sinuous music. He appeared to be listening to it.

'I don't know what to make of it all,' he said after a lengthy pause. 'Perhaps MacKinnon forgave me in the end. Perhaps he was merely reinhabiting his feelings of filial devotion.' He drummed his fingers on the arm of the chair. 'I don't know, I just don't know. Somehow, though, it was enough for me to get along, to put the past behind.' He laughed sadly. 'It seems that by merely telling this story I convict myself of a crime more heinous than murder. What that is, I'm not quite sure. The crime of which all who outlive their passions are convicted, I suppose. The crime of having failed to give our all . . . because in every life, you see, there is that opportunity for ultimate sacrifice. Perhaps the Greeks and the Romans had it right: to die nobly is the only worthy goal. Wasn't that their belief? No matter. Some tribe of fools must have believed it once, and in believing it, they must have won through to a form of brave wisdom. MacKinnon, now . . . This wasn't a noble death in the classic sense, but it seemed a noble expiration at any rate. Ah!' He smacked his palm against his thigh. 'I'm babbling. You see, that's my problem. I've lived this tremendous story . . . stories. God, I could tell you others that would equally amaze. And it – '

He broke off and stared into the middle distance. The piping was growing louder, more frantic. It was music like the whirling of smoke and the droning of insects, its cadences erratic, organic, and its melody elusive, always evolving.

'There!' Barnett leaned forward, gripping his knees. 'That says exactly what I'm driving at, that bloody wailing. You can't hum the melody, you can't keep it in mind, and, once it's ended, you can't recall it except in the most generic of senses. It's the same with MacKinnon's story. With most stories concerning this part of the world.' He slumped back in the chair like a puppet come unstrung. 'I keep feeling I should have learned something . . . and at times I think I have. I think I've learned enough to put a seal on things, to say this is the unremarkable and unredeemable world, the world of crows and silences, of mummies and vultures and sick hearts. It seems absolutely true. But then I'll remember something that puts the lie to it. The *maidan*, or MacKinnon's face at the end, all silvery and alive with calm expectancy, a ghost on fire with his last walk. Or something else, something from that place of the river and the city. Then everything I thought I knew, all my existential pronouncements and pithy morals become as vacuous as a preacher's homily. And all my satisfactions, my accommodations with the past, with guilt and betrayal,

159

they too seem empty.' He pursed his lips and blew out a forceful breath. 'I simply don't know anything. There's nothing I can hold, nothing I can depend on, not even the nastiest of apparent truths.' He cocked his head to the side. 'Listen,' he said, and made an amused noise. 'You can almost hear it . . . the one true commandment of the East. Thou must exult in the ineluctable, thou must dance to comprehend and understand nothing of stillness, thou must know only love, and love only knowledge.'

The music soared, sounding at one moment whining and horrid, and at the next lovely and serpentine, approaching a theme yet never stating it, conjuring a myriad of emotions – sadness, joy, lust, rage – yet never allowing them to exist for longer than it took to apprehend them, dispersing them in a flurry of notes or the idiot trilling of an atonal scale, then building again into a seductive weave. It was perfect and without form, that music; it had no true beginning, it had simply started up, and its end would not be a finale, but a mere stoppage of breath. It was the living East: it embodied the tin roofs, the orange-peel litter, the markets reeking of faeces and spice, the temples, the soldiers, the apes, the dictators, the old men, the child whores, the ghosts, the beggars, the expatriates, the Stone Age primitives, the Communists, the bleak capitalist skyscrapers – blending the whole awful, beautiful mix into a thin green confluence like a trickle of ditch water down a dark, muddy alley. The animals who drank from it had crazy dreams and died of fevers, the insects who swam in it were blind and malformed, yet in certain cases, in the cases of men like MacKinnon and Barnett, a single drop might seem to offer a cure for all the diseases of the West.

Barnett's fingers kneaded the arms of his chair, his expression intent as the music reached a crescendo, losing all coherence in a frenzy of twisted screeches and keenings. 'My God!' he said with awe, with despair, with yearning, as if he heard within that chaos the ringing of a sweet and secret bell, the elegant hint of some ungraspable mystical order. 'My God, will you just listen to that!'

160